WISHED

LISSA EVANS

www.davidficklingbooks.com

WISHED

LISSA EVANS

David Fickling Books

31 Beaumont Street
Oxford OX1 2NP, UK

Wished
is a
DAVID FICKLING BOOK

First published in Great Britain in 2022 by
David Fickling Books,
31 Beaumont Street,
Oxford, OX1 2NP

978-1-78845-202-1

1 3 5 7 9 10 8 6 4 2

DAVID FICKLING BOOKS Reg. No. 8340307

A CIP catalogue record for this book is available from the British Library.

Typeset in 13/17pt Dante by Falcon Oast Graphic Art Ltd.
Printed and bound in Great Britain by Clays Ltd, Elcograf S.p.A.

For Isotta

THEN

55 YEARS AGO

That year there was no party, and no cake, because no one felt like celebrating, but Rosanna still lined up her cards on the mantelpiece, so that it felt a bit like a birthday. There was one from her grandmother, with a picture of a girl stroking a kitten, and one from her aunt and uncle, with a picture of a girl stroking a puppy, and one from her other aunt and uncle with a picture of a girl not stroking anything, but just standing in a flowery meadow, smiling and holding a daisy chain.

Though the cards were very nice, Rosanna would secretly have preferred a picture of a girl steering a red-sailed boat across a tropical sea towards a mystery island, like the illustration on the front of the adventure storybook she'd been given as her best present.

Her favourite card was the one from her mum and

dad, and she put it in the middle of the mantelpiece. On the front, the words:

were illustrated as if they were bursting fireworks, lighting up a dark sky dusted with stars. Inside was a verse:

> *Ten candles on your birthday cake*
> *Each one's a wish for you to make –*
> *Adventures all, they wait for you*
> *To come and make those dreams come true.*

But there'd be no wishes this year. She put the birthday candles in a little box and placed them in a drawer.

Maybe next year, she thought.

After all, she had plans; lots of plans.

NOW

CHAPTER 1

'Miss *Filey's* house?' repeated Ed, outraged. 'We have to spend every day this week at Miss *Filey's* house? Are you totally serious?'

'Sorry, but it can't be helped,' said his dad, avoiding Ed's gaze and sidling out of the door.

'IT CAN'T BE HELPED,' echoed Ed's mother loudly, from the other room, where she was packing DVDs into a box. 'IT'S NO GOOD MOANING, ED.'

'I'm not moaning, I've hardly said anything – but can't we discuss it? Don't I have a say?'

'NOT IN THIS CASE,' called his mother. 'SORRY. YOU'LL JUST HAVE TO GRIN AND BEAR IT. THERE IS LITERALLY NO ALTERNATIVE, AND

IF MISS FILEY HADN'T MADE THE SUGGESTION,
I DON'T KNOW WHAT WE'D HAVE DONE.'

'But I'd rather spend next week in the shed. I'd rather spend it in the middle of a car park. In the rain. I bet she doesn't even have WiFi.'

'Who are you talking about?' asked his nine-year-old sister, Roo. She had an irritating habit of quietly entering rooms and then speaking before you even realized she was standing next to you.

Ed swivelled to face her. 'Sit down, Roo, I've got bad news.'

Her pointed face seemed to sharpen. 'Are you all right?' she asked.

'Yes, fine,' he said dismissively. 'It's not that sort of bad news. It's about the half-term holiday club. It's been cancelled.'

'Why?'

'The toilet at the hall overflowed and the building's been declared a biohazard and they're having to get specialist cleaners in. And so—'

'Why did it overflow?'

'No idea.' It was another of Roo's irritating habits to interrupt good stories with unimportant questions. 'So anyway, the club's not on, and for some reason we can't stay in the house when Mum and Dad are at work.'

'YOU KNOW EXACTLY WHY YOU CAN'T,' called their mother, who had bat-like hearing. 'THE WHOLE BACK OF OUR HOUSE IS BEING TORN OFF FOR THE NEW EXTENSION, SO THERE'LL BE WORK-MEN EVERYWHERE AND CABLES, AND THEY DON'T NEED CHILDREN WANDERING AROUND.'

'I don't *wander*.'

'AND ANYWAY YOU'RE BOTH TOO YOUNG TO STAY ON YOUR OWN, DON'T ARGUE, ED, OR I SHALL GO MAD.'

'So, what *are* we going to do?' asked Roo. 'Can we go to our cousins?' she added hopefully.

'THEY'RE AWAY,' called their mum.

'This is where the bad news comes in,' said Ed. 'Dad has done something completely random. He bumped into Miss Filey at the recycling bins this morning and she suggested that we go to her house during the day. For an entire week.'

'DON'T EXAGGERATE,' called Mum. 'YOU DON'T HAVE TO GO AT THE WEEKEND, SO IT'S LITERALLY FIVE DAYS.'

'Miss Filey?' asked Roo.

'Yes. Unbelievable, isn't it?'

'I've never been inside her house,' said Roo.

'Nor me. Why would anyone want to?'

'Well . . . it might be interesting.' Roo said the last few words quietly; she never enjoyed contradicting Ed, who was a year and a half older than her, because Ed enjoyed arguing and was good at it, and she didn't, and wasn't. But Miss Filey's house, at the bottom of the road, was intriguing. All the other houses were small and quite new, but hers was large and quite old; a broad, brick bungalow in a wide, square garden filled with flowering bushes and surrounded by trees. The front door was set in a deep porch, and above it was a window shaped like a fan. Reflections danced across it when you walked past.

'But even if it's interesting, it'll still contain Miss Filey,' said Ed. He leaned forward from the waist and opened his mouth wide, pitching his voice to an enthusiastic shriek. *'Super weather, isn't it?'*

'ARE YOU DOING AN IMPRESSION OF MISS FILEY?' called Mum.

'Yes, but it's not unkind, just accurate. *Have a simply smashing day!'* he added.

And it was true, thought Roo – that was exactly how Miss Filey talked: like somebody out of a black-and-white film. And she never stopped to have a conversation, but just trilled a comment as she hurried by, as if she was calling from a passing ship.

'SHE'S ALWAYS VERY KIND,' shouted their mum. 'REMEMBER SHE CAME TO THE FUNDRAISER AND BOUGHT EVERYTHING ON THE PLANT STALL AND ALL THE SMASHED BISCUITS IN THAT TIN THAT GOT DROPPED.'

'But what will we do there?' asked Ed, who didn't like talking about the fundraiser. 'I mean, seriously, Mum – what will we do at Miss Filey's house? Talk about the weather for five days? Eat broken biscuits?'

He waited for an answer, but there was no response from the next room.

'It might be OK,' said Roo.

'It won't. It'll be mind-numbingly boring.'

But Ed was wrong, because what happened at Miss Filey's house wasn't boring.

What happened at Miss Filey's house was beyond imagination.

CHAPTER 2

The front door opened the second that Roo put her finger on the bell, and she stepped back in shock and banged her heel on the footplate of Ed's wheelchair.

'Crikey, you're punctual!' said Miss Filey, who must have been waiting directly behind the door. 'Come on in.'

'Hi,' said Roo, standing on one leg and rubbing the other. 'Thank you for having us. We've brought packed lunches because there's loads of stuff Ed won't eat.'

'Allergies,' said Ed, who didn't have any allergies but who was incredibly picky. 'I don't need help,' he added quickly, as Miss Filey reached out for the wheelchair handles. 'I can do it myself.' There was only a shallow step, and he rolled across the doormat and onto the patterned wooden floor of the large, square hall. His first impression was that it was full of people, and then he realized that he was looking at a wide gilt-edged mirror that filled half of the opposite wall. His own face was only visible from the chin upwards, with the top half of Roo in a red sweatshirt just beside him, her straight dark hair swinging as she looked around the hall, and then, towering over both of them, their hostess.

Miss Filey was slender and quite tall, but she stooped slightly as if she felt awkward about her height. Her grey shoulder-length hair was pulled back on one side with a tortoiseshell clip, and she was wearing, as always, a knitted jumper and a plain knee-length skirt, so that she looked a bit like an elderly schoolgirl.

'I'm really jolly pleased you could come,' she announced.

'Thanks,' said Roo, still looking around. Everything looked old. Not 'old' as in 'your antique table is worth THREE THOUSAND POUNDS', but 'old' as in a TV series about men who smoked pipes and listened to the radio while their wives mended socks. There was an uncomfortable-looking chair beneath the mirror, with a little table beside it, for the telephone. There was a framed painting of a wonky cottage with roses climbing up the wall. In one corner, there was a tall wicker basket containing an umbrella, and in the other, a revolting stuffed tabby cat, its fur in matted clumps.

'That's Attlee,' said Miss Filey.

The stuffed cat opened its eyes, and Roo screamed rather loudly. 'Sorry,' she said.

'He's quite harmless,' said Miss Filey, 'and my father always said he was very intelligent and could understand every word we say.'

Attlee flicked them a slitted look and then yawned; the terrible stench of cat food and rotten teeth drifted across the hall. Ed covered his nose.

'He's frightfully old – nearly twenty-two!' said Miss Filey.

'Oh,' said Roo, trying to sound impressed.

There was a pause. Instead of telling them what to do, in the traditional way of grown-ups, Miss Filey remained standing in the centre of the hall, her hands clasped.

'Can we look around?' asked Roo, after a minute had passed.

'Gosh, what a terrific idea!' said Miss Filey. She

sounded rather relieved; Roo had the feeling that if the suggestion hadn't been made, they'd have spent the entire day standing in the hall.

Despite having no upstairs to it, Miss Filey's house felt at least twice the size of Ed and Roo's; all the rooms were large and square and light, and were linked by a broad corridor; despite this, Roo found something dispiriting about it. It was all very clean and tidy, but despite being full of furniture and ornaments, it somehow felt empty.

'So, this was my bedroom when I was a child,' said Miss Filey, opening yet another door. 'And now it's my little library.' This room was quite different to all the others: the only furniture was a chair and a desk with a globe on it. Floor-to-ceiling shelves on three walls held rows of large books and yellow-spined magazines, while on the fourth wall, next to the window, was a vast map of the world. Miss Filey paused to look at it. 'I try to learn the name of a new place every week,' she said, running a finger down the coast of Finland and then dabbing at a tiny island. 'This week it's Kirjalansaari, which is really jolly hard to say.'

'Could I ask you something?' said Ed. 'Do you have WiFi?'

Miss Filey looked thoughtful. 'Why. Fy.' she repeated,

rather carefully, as if the words were in another language. 'Now, is that a special sort of biscuit?'

Ed had been opening his backpack to get out his tablet, but he closed it again. 'Never mind,' he said.

'Do you have a TV?' asked Roo.

'Yes – it's in the living room, come and see.'

The television was about the size of a washing machine and looked as if it was made of wood. Miss Filey pressed a button. For a while nothing happened, and then the surprisingly small screen turned from dark grey to light grey and there was a faint whining noise. 'I can't remember the last time I turned it on – my father used to enjoy watching history programmes,' she said. 'While it's warming up, would you like to have a look at the garden?'

It wasn't until they had followed the flagstoned path as far as the back wall that Roo risked a look at Ed. His expression made her snort with laughter.

'Glad you think it's funny,' he said. 'That television should have police tape around it. I'm surprised it didn't explode when she switched it on.'

'She's quite nice though, isn't she?' said Roo. 'In a weird sort of way.'

They both looked back towards the house, as if Miss Filey might be listening, but there was nothing to see except the open French windows, and beyond them the faint glow of the television still warming up.

Somewhere, in another garden, a dog was woofing.

'Hi,' said a voice, behind them.

CHAPTER 3

An extremely short kid of about Ed's age was looking at them over the low garden wall. He had a huge gap between his teeth and was cross-eyed.

'Hello,' said Roo, trying to sound both friendly and sympathetic. 'What's your name?'

'Elastico,' said the boy.

'Sorry?'

'Elastico.'

'It can't be.'

'Yes, it can, because that is my *superpower*.' And as the boy spoke he suddenly grew taller, but slightly jerkily so it was obvious that he'd actually been on his knees behind the wall. He also uncrossed his eyes and took a small square of dark paper off his front teeth, revealing himself to be completely ordinary-looking.

'Hi, I'm Willard,' he said, grinning. 'Did I fool you?'

'Slightly,' said Ed, unwillingly impressed by the amount of effort that had gone into the introduction. 'Do you always do that when you meet new people?'

'I've got a range of things,' said Willard. 'Eyepatch, fake sick, spider crawling up my face, that sort of thing.'

'Why?' asked Roo.

'Just, you know . . .' Willard shrugged 'For a laugh. I'm class clown. What's your names?'

'I'm Ed and this is my sister, Roo.'

'It's "Lucy", really,' said Roo.

'How do you get "Roo" from "Lucy"?'

'I couldn't say her name properly when I was little,' said Ed, 'and it just stuck.'

'Though I do quite like being called "Lucy",' said Roo.

'Is that thing electric?' asked Willard, nodding at the wheelchair.

'No.'

'Why are you in it?'

'Hurt my leg,' said Ed, briefly and untruthfully.

'We've just moved here,' said Willard. 'The day before yesterday. From Wales.'

'You don't sound Welsh,' said Ed.

'I'm not. Before that we were in Northampton. We're always moving, because my mother owns a circus.'

'Really?' asked Roo, astonished.

'No, just kidding, she's a vicar.'

'Oh.'

'What does your mum do?' asked Willard.

'She's a driving instructor. So's our dad.'

'And which school are you at?'

'Meadows Primary,' said Ed.

'That's where I'll be going too, after the holiday. Are you in Year Five?'

Ed nodded.

'Me too,' said Willard. 'I'm class clown,' he said again, as if it were an official title.

Ed felt a stir of irritation. Making people laugh was his own speciality, though he tended to do it with sarcasm rather than fake sick.

'Who's that?' asked Willard, looking past them. 'What's she holding?'

Ed and Roo turned to see Miss Filey coming through the French windows with a small gong in her hand. 'The television is ON,' she announced, hitting the gong with a drumstick.

'She's called Miss Filey,' said Roo. 'We're spending the day with her.'

'Can I too?' asked Willard, already slinging a leg over the wall.

'Umm . . .' said Roo, just as Willard lifted up the other leg and fell heavily into a shrub. He lay on the ground beneath it, eyes shut, mouth open, one hand twitching slightly.

'We ought to ask her first,' said Ed. 'And shouldn't you check with someone at home?'

Willard opened his eyes. 'How did you know I wasn't badly injured?'

'Lucky guess.'

Willard stood up. 'I'll just come in for five minutes. Hello, Miss Filey,' he said, walking straight past her. 'I'm a friend of Ed and Roo's. Holy *cow*!!' he exclaimed, staggering back at the sight of the TV.'

'It's old,' said Roo, stating the obvious.

'It's *black* and *white*,' said Willard, gazing mesmerized at the screen, where two men in suits were standing in a studio. The top half of the picture was stationary while the bottom half kept jerking around, as if the presenters were doing a Charleston.

'There's lemonade and biscuits,' said Miss Filey, placing a tray on a spindly-looking table with a scratched top. 'I'll try and buy a packet of Why Fy for tomorrow. Do make yourself at home, everyone.'

'Thanks very much,' said Roo. She watched Ed fiddling with the control buttons, which stuck out of the set like biro tops, and then she realized that Miss Filey was lingering next to the door, her smile slightly fixed, as if waiting for something. 'Thanks very much,' she said again, and Miss Filey ducked her head in an awkward nod, and left the room.

The television turned out only to have two channels, and both were covered in fizzy white dots, and the boys soon lost interest. For no particular reason, Willard put four biscuits in his mouth at the same time, started to choke and then accidentally kicked over his lemonade while coughing. Ed threw a cushion onto the mess, and Roo looked for something to wipe it up with. There was a cabinet on one side of the room, and she searched through the drawers; there were beautiful tablecloths, as perfect as if they'd just been woven, and embroidered mats, fancy forks, a cake slice with a china handle and a small tin box with a hinged lid, containing a bundle of little silver-and-white candles. In the bottom drawer, she found a packet of paper napkins and she opened it and soaked up as much of the lemonade as possible.

'Where's Willard gone?' she asked, suddenly realizing that he wasn't in the room.

Ed shrugged. 'He just ran off, back into the garden – maybe he's embarrassed about knocking the drink over. I tell you something, I'm really not looking forward to being in the same class as him.' There'd be no room for his own witty comments with Willard making armpit fart noises every three minutes.

'I'm back!' said Willard, slightly out of breath, bursting in through the French windows with a plate in one hand. On it was three-quarters of an iced cake, decorated with fizzy fish. 'It was my birthday yesterday – Mum said we could finish this off.'

'You haven't eaten much of it,' said Ed.

'Well, it was only me and Mum – I don't know anyone here yet, do I?'

'Oh . . .' Ed felt a tweak of pity; a birthday with no friends sounded pretty miserable. 'OK, yes, I'd love a slice.'

'There's some birthday candles in the drawer,' said Roo, going back to the cabinet. 'We could just use one, couldn't we? It would make it more special. And here's some matches,' she said, rummaging round and finding a box.

Willard put the cake on the spindly-legged table,

and Roo stuck one of the white-and-silver candles in the icing.

She was just about to light it when Willard puffed his cheeks, as if about to vomit. 'Something stinks in here,' he said.

Ed glanced round. 'It's the cat.' Attlee had stalked into the room, the fishy smell surrounding him like an invisible force field.

Roo struck the match. 'I like cats, but I do wish Miss Filey had a dog,' she said, lighting the candle, 'because I really love—'

There was a crash, and Attlee shot across the room like a thrown fish sandwich, his tail a plume of terror. He ran straight up the wall and clung to a framed embroidery of a vase of flowers, hissing over his shoulder at an enormous dog that had charged in through the open French windows from the garden. It was covered in tight brown curls and its mouth was open in a wide and toothy grin. Ed spun away; the dog's mouth was far too near his own face for comfort.

'It's a dog!' shouted Willard unnecessarily.

Attlee was making a terrible sing-song yowling, and the dog was up on its hind legs, pawing at the wall just beneath him. Roo grabbed its collar and pulled, and the dog gave a joyful sort of bound in her direction so that she stumbled back, knocking against the cake table. She let go of the collar and managed to grab the plate, but the cake itself was already mid-air. It hit the wall and disintegrated in a blizzard of crumbs. A fizzy fish pinged off the television screen.

Breathless, Roo turned round. The dog had gone.

'Golly Moses, what on earth is happening?' called Miss Filey, hurrying into the room.

'A neighbour's dog,' said Ed, cautiously spinning back round. 'We heard it woofing earlier. It's gone out again now. It was huge – it must have jumped the garden wall.'

'Sorry,' said Roo. 'About all the mess. It's Willard's cake – we'll clear it up.'

'Oh, it's only crumbs. I'll go and fetch the dustpan and brush,' said Miss Filey, struggling to detach Attlee's claws from the embroidered picture. 'I'll obviously have to be more careful about closing the doors. Are you all right?' she asked Willard, who was still standing on the sofa.

He nodded rather stiffly, but his eyes were as round as buttons, and when Miss Filey had taken the cat out of the room, he flapped his mouth a couple of times before he could speak. 'Did you see that?' he asked.

'Couldn't exactly miss it, could we?' said Ed.

'I don't mean the dog appearing. I mean it . . . disappearing. It was there and then it wasn't there.'

'It must have gone out through the French windows.'

'*No!*' said Willard, 'I was looking straight at it, and it was—' He snapped a finger. 'Gone. Into thin air. Like magic.'

'Sure,' said Ed, rolling his eyes at his sister.

But Roo said nothing at all.

CHAPTER 4

At home, there was dust everywhere, and sheets of dingy plastic taped across the place where the living-room wall had been.

'Well,' said Dad, trying to sound cheerful as he hoovered flakes of plaster off the carpet, 'the builders have made a start. Won't be too long now – just a month or two.'

It was going to be a ground-floor bedroom and bathroom for Ed. Currently he either had to go upstairs on his bum, or his dad had to carry him up, and once there, he couldn't use his wheelchair because the doorways were too narrow, which meant that he had to wobble around holding onto things, in a way that made him feel like a toddler. So he was looking forward to getting the new extension; the only trouble was that the whole of the small town they lived in seemed to be looking forward to it as well.

'I'm really sorry,' his mum had said. 'We just can't afford it without a bit of help.' So there had been local cake sales and sponsored hopping races and a talent show and a pie-throwing contest and now people he didn't even know said, 'Ed, my man!' in the street and gave him a high five or called out 'I bought six rock buns at the fundraiser – hope my contribution helped!' from the other side of the road, and Ed had to smile at them all.

'HOW WAS MISS FILEY?' shouted Mum from the kitchen.

'OK,' he said.

There was a pause.

'A LITTLE MORE DETAIL WOULD BE NICE,' called Mum.

'We met a boy called Willard who thinks he's funny. We found a cupboard full of jigsaws and started one with a lot of sky. We ate some slightly stale cake. I mean, the whole thing was *exactly* like going to Disneyland. Do we have to go back tomorrow?'

'YES, BUT MAYBE WE CAN MAKE SOME

OTHER ARRANGEMENT FOR THE END OF THE WEEK. LUCY'S VERY QUIET.'

'Hello, Mum,' called Roo. 'Yes, it was fine. Miss Filey's nice.' She spoke absently, her thoughts still circling the incident of the dog. She kept thinking of the moment that she'd grabbed it by the collar.

'WHAT'S HER HOUSE LIKE?'

'Old,' said Ed. 'But not necessarily in a good way.'

'It's big,' said Roo. 'Really big for one person.'

Mum appeared in the kitchen door, a potato masher in her hand. 'Miss Filey's father only died a few months ago – he was in his late nineties, I think, and he needed a lot of looking after. I'm not sure if she has any other family.'

'Nor me. Are we having sausage and mash?' asked Ed.

'Fish cakes.' Their mum went back into the kitchen.

'Ed,' said Roo. 'I have to tell you something.' She jerked her head towards the hall.

Ed followed her. 'What is it?' he asked, keeping his voice low.

'You know the dog?'

'Willard's Disappearing Dog, you mean?'

'Yes.'

'What about it?'

'There was a little tag on its collar. I saw it when I grabbed him.'

'OK. And?'

She took a deep breath. 'It said "49 Alum Road" on it. That's Miss Filey's address, isn't it? But Miss Filey doesn't have a dog.'

Ed waited.

'The thing is, when I lit the candle,' continued Roo, 'I said, "I do wish Miss Filey had a dog".'

Ed raised an eyebrow. 'So, what you're saying is that you made a wish and it came true?'

'Yes. And then when the candle went out, the wish ended, and the dog vanished.'

'We've only got Willard's word for that. We had our backs to it.'

'Well, OK, but . . . what if it really did disappear? What's the explanation?'

Ed folded his arms in a teacherish way. 'Let's look at this logically. As far as I can see, there are two possibilities. One is that you made a wish and it magically came true. And the other is that you slightly misread the print on a dog's collar and it didn't say forty-nine, it said another number, and the dog actually belonged to a neighbour and it jumped the garden wall. Which of those two possibilities is the most likely?' Ed saw his sister's shoulders droop with disappointment. 'You can always light another candle tomorrow,' he said, trying to cheer her up. 'Check out your theory.'

'But what would I wish for?'

Ed shrugged. 'How about something that definitely couldn't turn up in a normal living room?'

'An elephant? No, too big. A . . . a sloth? No, it might wee everywhere. A . . . a . . .'

'Sloths only urinate when it's raining,' said Ed, who knew nearly everything. 'Why don't you sleep on it,' he added. 'And at least Willard won't be there tomorrow.'

'Hello, youngsters!' said Miss Filey, when they arrived. 'I've left the jigsaw exactly the way it was, as I thought you'd want to carry on with it.'

'Thanks,' said Ed, giving a double thumbs up. 'We've been really looking forward to carrying on with that great big, blue, totally featureless sky.'

'Super,' said Miss Filey, missing the sarcasm. 'You'll find biscuits and lemonade waiting for you. And I'm just going to have a little look around in the shed for some other games.'

In the television room, the only reminders of the dog incident were a few loose threads hanging from the embroidery on the wall. Ed took a Jaffa Cake and used his teeth to peel the chocolate from the top.

'OK,' said Roo. 'I've thought and thought and I know exactly what I'm going to wish for.' She opened the drawer.

'Stick the candle in the orange jelly bit,' said Ed, offering his biscuit.

'Do you want to know my wish?' asked Roo.

'No, surprise me.'

She picked out a candle with fingers that were clumsy with excitement. 'It's quite fragile,' she said. Small flakes of silver and white wax dropped onto the Jaffa cake.

'I expect it's the same age as everything else in this house,' said Ed.

Roo took a match out of the box and struck it. The little blue flame sizzled into life.

'Are you sure you don't want to know my wish?' she asked.

'No,' said Ed, selecting a custard cream, 'that's OK.'

Roo held the match to the candle wick. When she spoke, her voice was high and nervous. 'I wish I had a tame ant that would obey commands.'

'What?' Ed turned to look at her, half a biscuit in his mouth. The candle flame shuddered and steadied.

'You said to choose something that definitely wouldn't turn up in a normal living room,' said Roo. 'But I thought we shouldn't ask for anything too noticeable in case Miss Filey came in.' She blew the match out and looked around carefully. 'Can you see it?'

'Your tame ant?'

'Yes. I suppose it could be anywhere – maybe I should have said "a tame ant in a box".'

As she spoke, the doorbell rang; there were footsteps in the hall, followed by Miss Filey's fluting tones, and another, softer, woman's voice. After a moment or two, the door to the television room opened and Willard walked in.

'Don't move!' ordered Roo.

'Why not? What are you doing? Is it someone else's birthday?'

'There's an ant somewhere and we mustn't squash it.'

'Bet you're wondering why I'm here,' said Willard.

'Not really,' said Ed.

'My mum came round to apologize to Miss Filey about me climbing over the wall yesterday, and Miss Filey said I could stay all today as well. Mum's always apologizing for me,' he added cheerfully. 'My gran says

I should have been christened "Sorry About Willard".
Oh, there's your ant,' he added, nodding at Roo.

'Where? *Where?*'

'On your hand,' said Willard. 'The right one.'

Roo looked at her palm, and then carefully turned her hand over. On the back of it was an ant.

It waved at her.

CHAPTER 5

'It waved at me!' said Roo. Astonishment fizzed up from the soles of her feet and surged through her like streams of bubbles. 'It *waved* at me!' She lifted her hand so that the ant was at eye level. 'Hello, Mrs Ant,' she said. 'And now walk backwards.'

The ant walked backwards.

She looked up and saw Willard's face just inches away – his eyes and mouth identical 'O's of astonishment.

'Sit up and beg,' said Roo to the ant. It did. 'Good ant,' she said, and her voice was shaking. 'Clever ant.'

Ed stared, his head thrust forward. He felt as if he'd been turned into scaffolding – every joint locked and frozen. He *couldn't* be seeing what he was seeing; it wasn't possible.

'Roll over,' said Roo. The ant rolled over and stood up again, waving its antennae.

'Do a dance!' ordered Willard. The ant performed what looked like the hokey-cokey and Willard and Roo let out near-identical squawks of amazement and laughter and Ed heard himself make a choking noise.

'That candle,' said Willard. 'You made a wish when you lit it! Like the dog.'

'Yes.' Roo was smiling so widely that the word sounded more like 'Ess'. The ant seemed to be waiting for instructions. 'Right,' she said, 'and now—'

Ed leaned forward and blew out the candle.

The ant disappeared.

'Oh!' said Roo. She stared at the back of her hand; she checked her palm, and her wrist and her sleeve, and the floor beneath and then she turned to look at Ed, her whole face crumpled with disappointment. 'You made it go!'

Ed's world seemed to tilt. He knew what he believed, and he knew what he'd just seen, and he felt as if he was sliding into a terrifying gap between the two.

'Why did you do that?' asked Roo. 'Why?'

'That was *mean*,' said Willard.

Ed lifted a hand to his mouth, and bit hard on the thumbnail. It hurt, and the world steadied. 'I wanted to prove that it was just an ordinary ant. I wanted to prove that it would still be there when the candle went out,' he said. 'I don't believe in magical things, only in science.'

'But it *was* magic, wasn't it?' asked Roo. 'Wasn't it? And you blew out the wish and now it's gone.' She was almost crying.

'I'm sorry, Roo,' said Ed. 'I'm really, really sorry. I don't know what else to say.'

She wiped her eyes and wouldn't look at him, but she nodded.

'I still think it was a mean thing to do,' said Willard. 'But I've got an idea. There's still a bit of the candle left – maybe we can get another wish out of it. Shall I give it a go?'

Roo nodded miserably. 'But wish for something different. I don't want to have to say goodbye to the ant *again*.'

'OK. I wish . . .' said Willard, striking a match and holding it to the small remaining stub of wax, 'I wish . . . I wish I had a million pounds!'

Nothing happened. The three of them sat looking at each other and then, after about thirty seconds, the candle flame wavered and fizzled out, leaving only a smear of wax and the black speck of the burned wick.

'It didn't work,' said Willard.

'You wouldn't have had time to spend it, anyway,' said Roo comfortingly.

'So, definitely just one wish per candle,' said Ed. He went over to the drawer, and took out the tin box, and arranged the contents in a row on the top of the cabinet. 'Eight left.'

'Eight wishes,' said Roo softly.

'Eight!' shouted Willard.

They were very small candles, thinner than a pencil and barely the length of Ed's little finger, and there was nothing unusual about them, except that the wax was so old that it was almost transparent.

'Why?' asked Ed, almost to himself. 'Why these?'

'Space Mountain!' said Willard, waving his arms. 'Riding an elephant! Pranking the Queen! Driving a Formula One car! Being famous! Flying!'

'Flying!' repeated Roo. 'Oh, let's start with flying.'

'Hang on,' said Ed. 'How long was the ant here for?'

'Three minutes? A bit more?' said Willard. 'Bungee jumping in the Grand Canyon! My own TV show!'

'Flying,' said Roo again.

'So, even if we let a whole candle burn down, the

total length of a wish isn't going to be more than about four and a half minutes. What's the point of having your own TV show for *four and a half minutes*?'

'Flying,' said Roo, for the third time. She looked at Ed. 'Please.'

And Ed, torn between curiosity and unshakeable doubt, took a candle and handed it to Roo.

She pushed it into the top of the Jaffa Cake, and lit a match.

'I wish we—' she began, and then paused. 'Should I say: "I wish we had wings"?' she asked.

'No,' said Ed quickly. He still didn't quite believe in what was happening, but he wasn't prepared to risk the three of them trying to take off from Miss Filey's back garden, with all the neighbours watching. Besides, 'wings' might mean anything – he had a sudden vision of Willard flapping a great pair of leathery dragon wings and knocking all the pictures off the walls. 'We've only got four and a half minutes, remember. You don't want to spend half of that working out how to take off.'

'How about you say, "I wish we were *flying*",' said Willard cunningly. 'Then we'd have already done the take-off bit.'

'All right,' said Roo, holding the match to the wick. 'I wish we were—'

'No!' shouted Ed, his thoughts jumping ahead. But Roo had already spoken the final word. The flame leaped.

And – with no break in time whatsoever, no sense of movement, no flash, no pow, no zap, no zing – they were flying.

CHAPTER 6

'Tea, coffee, orange juice?' asked a flight attendant.
They stared at her.

'No? A biscuit, then?'

Automatically, Ed held out a hand. The flight attendant gave him a single, plastic-wrapped shortbread and carried on pushing her trolley down the aisle.

'Massive disappointment,' said Willard. '*Massive*. We're not even in first class.'

'I tried to stop it,' said Ed, eating the biscuit. 'I shouted "No", but you didn't listen, Roo.'

Roo could hardly speak from disappointment. She'd imagined herself twisting through the air like a swallow, and now here she was in the middle seat in a cramped aeroplane and all she could see outside the window was cloud.

'But being in an aeroplane's still good though,' said Willard. 'We might be on our way to an amazing destination.'

'Yes, we might,' said Ed. 'We'll all have a brilliant time as long as we manage to touch down and go through immigration without passports in under three minutes.'

'Oh, yeah,' said Willard, his smile fading. 'Still, you know what – it was a wish and it came true. We *are* flying, and if you think about it, that's like totally incredibubble.'

'You mean "incredible",' said Ed.

'Yes, but it's funnier if you say "incredibubble".'

'It really isn't.'

'So what should we have wished for, then?' asked Roo quickly. She could see Ed teetering on the edge of crossness, and she thought it might partly be because no one had listened to him, and partly because he was stuck on a plane without his wheelchair. He always got irritable if he had to depend on other people for getting about.

'I don't know,' said Ed, but his expression grew thoughtful as he turned the question over in his mind.

'I think we need to wish for something quite precise. Something that's wonderful from the minute you arrive, so you don't waste a single second of a brilliant experience.'

There was a pause.

From the row in front of them came a loud snore.

'I wish I'd said yes to a biscuit now,' said Willard.

Roo stared out of the window. There was literally nothing to see.

'This seems longer than four and a half minutes,' she said.

'Boring things always seem long,' said Ed.

Willard was looking through the pocket on the back of the next seat. 'I know what we should do,' he said. 'We should take—'

And without warning, they were back – back at Miss Filey's, and a wisp of smoke was curling up from the Jaffa Cake, and a pool of wax was beginning to harden on the top of it.

'—a souvenir!' announced Willard, waving something.

'That's an airline sick bag,' said Ed.

'Yeah, but it's, like, a *special* sick bag. I'm going to save it.'

'For some special sick?'

There was a rap at the door, and Willard went to open it.

'I've found quite a decent lot of games in the shed,' said Miss Filey, entering with her arms full of boxes. 'Though they're frightfully dusty.' She sneezed a couple of times and set the pile down on the cabinet.

'Thank you,' said Roo.

She waited for Miss Filey to say something else, or to leave, but their hostess stayed where she was, her hands still on the boxes, her head bent. Seconds went by.

Roo glanced, frowning, at her brother; his puzzled expression mirrored her own.

'Are you all right, Miss Filey?' asked Ed.

Miss Filey took a sudden deep breath. 'Oh, gosh,' she said, in an odd voice. She fumbled with her sleeve and took out a handkerchief. 'Golly,' she said, and blew her nose. 'Sorry to be such a soppy dishrag – I hadn't seen these for such a very long time. You found them in the drawer, did you?'

Delicately, she picked up one of the candles that Ed had lined up on the cabinet, and as she looked at it, her expression softened so that despite the wrinkles she looked very young. 'These were bought for my tenth birthday party,' she said.

'Why didn't they get used?' asked Willard.

Ed pulled a warning face at him. No one would look the way that Miss Filey was looking now, if this had been a happy story.

'It's quite all right,' said Miss Filey, catching his expression and trying to smile. 'I don't mind answering. The day before my birthday, my mother suddenly became terribly ill, and had to be rushed to hospital, and of course the party was cancelled, and she hadn't made the cake and no one felt like eating one anyway. She was there for weeks and weeks, and my father was trying to manage on his own, and it was all the most miserable muddle.'

'And did your mother . . .' Roo hardly dared to ask. 'I mean, did she get better?'

'Oh, yes,' said Miss Filey more brightly. 'Yes, eventually – a bit better, anyway – but even when she came home, she was never completely well again. At first we had a nurse, but when I was old enough to leave school, I was able to stay at home and look after her myself.'

'Didn't you want to go out to work?' asked Willard. 'Or to college?'

'Well, I was needed at home, you see, so it was out of the question.'

'Oh.'

'But she was lovely, my mother,' said Miss Filey. 'And it didn't matter so much that I couldn't go away, because I made penfriends all over the world.'

'What are penfriends?' asked Roo.

'People I exchange letters with, though we've never met.'

'What, actual letters you write with an actual *pen*?' asked Willard, amazed.

'Yes, that's right. And I built up my own little library of maps and books, so whenever I got a letter, or I studied the books, I felt just like an explorer.'

But despite Miss Filey's words, her expression was wistful, and Roo felt her own skin prickle all over, as if guilt was a swarm of mosquitoes. They had used Miss Filey's house and investigated her garden and eaten her biscuits and poked around in her cupboards and their hostess might as well have been a cardboard cut-out, labelled 'NEIGHBOUR', for all the notice they'd taken of her – and yet Miss Filey was a real person, who had once been a child herself, who had lived a life that wasn't, perhaps, the life she had wanted to live. An indoor life.

And Roo remembered seeing her on that first day, standing with a fixed smile as if she'd just walked into a party where she didn't know anyone, and it occurred to her suddenly that Miss Filey was *shy*! And the idea was amazing: that a grown-up with a loud voice might not be as confident as she looked.

Roo raised a hand. 'It was me,' she said. 'I found the candles because I was looking in the drawer for something to wipe up a spill and it was my idea to light them and now we've used three of them and I'm so sorry. I should have asked.'

'It was all of us,' said Ed, and Willard nodded.

'Golly, they were only candles,' said Miss Filey. 'I don't mind. Really.'

'But they're special candles,' said Willard. 'Like, *outstandingly* special.'

'Well, perhaps. I remember spending a great deal of time that year thinking about birthday wishes. I'd been given a smashing book of adventure stories that I read over and over again, and I used my favourites as inspiration. Gosh, it's all coming back to me now! I had wishes like travelling on a rocket to the moon, or inheriting a zoo, or rescuing people trapped in an avalanche. And because we couldn't go out very much, I used to daydream that all these wishes happened right in the house. I'd stand in the hall and decide which story I wanted to visit – I'd imagine that my bedroom would become a film studio, or I'd find the entrance to a cave in the linen cupboard, or the pond in the garden would turn into a limitless sea, so I could sail to my very own island in a little boat with a red sail. Anyhow . . .' Miss Filey blew her nose again, loudly and with great finality. 'Perhaps you'd like to look through these games? And I shall go and—'

Without finishing her sentence, she left the room rather quickly.

For a long time, no one spoke. Carefully – very, very carefully – Ed put the remaining seven candles back in their tin box in the drawer. His fingers sparkled with tiny fragments of silver wax.

Roo pulled her sleeve over her hand and gave the pile of games a dusting.

Willard lifted the lid of the top one, and looked at the folded board, and the jumble of chess pieces within. He let the lid drop again.

The three of them looked at each other.

'We've got to tell her,' said Roo. 'Haven't we?'

CHAPTER 7

'You're quiet,' said Willard's mother, that evening.

'What?' asked Willard.

'You're *quiet*,' shouted his mum; this time Willard took off his headphones.

'I'm watching a science tutorial.'

'Really?'

'It's called "Twenty Things to do with Chewing Gum that you've Never Done Before".'

'Oh.'

'But I was thinking incredibly hard about something, as well. Can I ask you a hyper . . . thetty . . . thing question?'

His mother had been editing a sermon on her

laptop, but now she stopped and looked at him, her head tilted like a dog that's just heard the faint clink of a lead being lifted. 'You mean "hypothetical?" As in, "a question about something that hasn't happened, but which might happen"?'

'Yes.'

'Have you been' – his mother's face filled with hope – *'reading*?'

'No. Ed at Miss Filey's house said it. The sarcastic one in the wheelchair.'

'Oh yes, Ed Crane. Someone I was visiting today was talking about him.'

'About how sarcastic he is?'

'No, about why he's in a wheelchair.'

'He hurt his leg,' said Willard.

There was a pause; his mother seemed to notice a spot on the laptop screen and gave it a rub with her thumb. 'Weren't you going to ask a hypothetical question?' she asked.

'Yes.'

'Go on then, I'm listening.' She leaned forward and clasped her hands; her expression, as usual, was serious and sympathetic, her eyes fixed on his. Sometimes, Willard thought, it might be easier to talk to her if she looked a bit *less* serious and sympathetic.

'OK,' he said. 'What if something unbeliev-able happened, and it only happened because you'd borrowed something from somebody without telling them – would you owe it to that person to show them the unbelievable thing, even if they might drop dead from the total unbelievability of it?'

His mother blinked a couple of times. *'Drop dead?'*

'Like from the shock. Would that be murder? If the person was like really, really old.'

His mother's face cleared. 'By "really, really old", do you mean Miss Filey?'

'Yes.'

'Because I'd say she's only in her mid-sixties, which isn't what I'd call "really, really old". And she looks perfectly healthy to me. There've been plenty of sci-entists and writers and artists and reformers who achieved their greatest work in their sixties.'

'So not "really, really old"?' said Willard thoughtfully.

'No.'

'Only *"quite* old".'

His mother took a breath as if to carry on discuss-ing the subject, and then let it out with a sigh and shook her head. She did this quite often when talking to Willard.

'Could you repeat the rest of the hypothetical question?' she asked. 'Because I think I need to hear it again.'

'It doesn't matter,' said Willard. 'What you just said was helpful.'

'Was it?' His mother looked both puzzled and gratified. 'Well . . . good.' She watched Willard put on his headphones again. 'It's lovely to see you concentrate on something,' she said.

Ed and Roo were in Ed's bedroom, trying to make a list.

'OK,' said Ed. 'So, these are our criteria for a potential wish to show Miss Filey how the candles work: *One.* Something that definitely couldn't happen in real life, so that the only possible explanation would be that it's . . . you know . . .'

'Magic,' supplied Roo, who wasn't embarrassed by the word.

'. . . and *Two*,' continued Ed, 'something that won't terrify her. So, I think it should be a smallish wish, in the TV room, so she can be sitting down when it happens, and then if she faints she won't get hurt.'

'We could have the ant back,' suggested Roo hopefully.

'I think we need something larger, more definite. But not frightening.'

'What about something fairly ordinary appearing that wasn't there before?' said Roo. 'Like a new TV. Except that she's not very interested in TVs.'

'We could ask her!' said Ed. 'We could say: what have you always wanted in this room? And then let *her* wish for it. She'd have to believe it then.'

Roo nodded. 'Brilliant,' she said. 'That's brilliant. That's what we'll do.'

The next morning, they waited until Miss Filey brought them the usual 10 a.m. lemonade and biscuits. Attlee the cat had followed her into the room and was winding around her ankles, making the sort of noise that's often written as 'miaow' but which actually sounded more like someone with a sore throat attempting to break the world burping record. The usual appalling smell moved through the room with him.

'I don't know what's wrong with Attlee today,' said Miss Filey. 'He's been following me from room to room all morning.' She turned to go, and Ed nudged Roo.

'Miss Filey,' she said.

'Yes, Lucy?'

'We want to ask you something. Could you sit down?'

'Oh!' Miss Filey looked slightly flustered. 'Is it about the refreshments? I still haven't been able to find a packet of Why Fy for you. Do you think I should look in the cake aisle at the supermarket?'

'It's not that – it's about the birthday candles.'

'Oh,' said Miss Filey again, more softly. She sat down on the sofa next to Willard and folded her hands in her lap. For a moment or two no one spoke. Ed looked at Roo, Roo looked at Willard and Willard crossed his eyes.

'OK,' said Ed, taking responsibility, because somebody had to. 'We've got something we want to show you. But only if you don't mind if we use another of the candles. Do you mind?'

'No, not at all.'

Roo jumped up and went over to the cabinet.

'I forgot to tell you – I brought something,' said Willard. He took a small piece of silver foil out of his pocket and unwrapped it to reveal a blob of chewing gum. 'We could stick the candle to a plate with this,' he said.

'Has that been in your mouth?' asked Ed. 'It's quite a good idea, though,' he added grudgingly, 'as long as you're the only one who touches it.'

Roo stacked the biscuits next to the plate, and Willard put the blob of chewing gum in the middle and pushed the candle into it.

'The thing is,' said Ed to Miss Filey. 'We've discovered that these candles aren't ordinary candles.'

'They've got superpowers,' said Willard.

'Golly,' said Miss Filey, looking baffled.

'We'll show you,' continued Ed. 'Can you think of something you'd like to change about this room? For instance, would you like a . . . a pot plant in the corner? Or a new ornament or something?'

Miss Filey looked around the room as if she hadn't seen it for years. 'Gosh,' she said, 'I'm so used to it that I've never thought very much about changing things – I grew up with all this furniture. Do you see that long scratch on the little side table? I accidentally did that with a dolly's tea set made of tin, when I was about six. I've always felt rather guilty about it.'

'That's it!' exclaimed Ed.

Miss Filey looked startled, and Attlee the cat tipped his head back and let out another grating screech.

'It's perfect,' said Ed, handing the matches to Miss Filey. 'All you need to do is light the candle and while you're lighting it, say, "I wish that scratch on the table had gone".'

Miss Filey took the matches, her expression doubtful.

'That's all you need to say,' said Roo encouragingly.

'Is it . . . a game?' asked Miss Filey. 'Do I get a forfeit if I do it wrong?'

'It's a *bit* like a game,' said Roo. 'A wishing game. But no forfeits.'

'So as I light it, I have to say "I wish that scratch on the table had gone"?'

'Yes.'

Miss Filey drew herself upright in the chair and struck the match. Attlee let out a long, furious 'NNYYYAAAHHHRRR' accompanied by a dab of the paw which caught and laddered Miss Filey's tights.

'I wish the scratch on the table had gone,' said Miss Filey, holding the match to the candle wick – which was taking a long while to light – 'though actually, I think what I *really* wish is that I knew what was wrong with the cat.' The wick caught and flamed.

'You want to know what's wrong with me?' asked Attlee. 'Oh, where on earth do I start? My life is one long *nightmare*.'

breast poached in a light broth, with a side plate of duck-liver pâté and a freshly grilled salmon garnished with shrimps, but if you feel you must open a *pouch*, then the Haddock and Sprat flavour will be adequate.'

'Good,' said Miss Filey. 'Now, could I ask you something? What happened to my thimble that I saw you playing with last week?'

'It's under the fridge,' said Attlee. 'Any more questions? I'm feeling rather tired. You may have forgotten, but I was almost killed by a dog earlier this week.' He yawned and they all leaned backwards to avoid his breath.

'I've got one,' said Willard. 'What does a mouse taste like?'

'Similar to a hamster but not as juicy.'

'What's it feel like to purr?' asked Roo.

'Like having your head massaged from the inside. How much longer is this going on for? I'm beginning to think that speech is overrated.'

Ed looked at the candle; only a little stub was left. 'About half a minute,' he said.

'Final question, then,' said Attlee.

'When this wish ends,' said Ed slowly, 'can you give us a sign if you can remember talking to us?'

'A sign?'

'Yes, something you wouldn't usually do, like' – Ed looked around for inspiration – 'going to the jigsaw box and taking out a piece of sky.'

Attlee twitched the end of his tail. 'Why?'

'Because then we'd know for certain that you can understand speech, even if you can't speak yourself.'

'I'll consider it,' said Attlee. 'I *might* do that, but then again, I might *MYAAAAAAAAAGH*.' A thin wisp of smoke signalled the candle's end, and Attlee's speech turned into the usual scraping yowl.

There was a moment of silence and then Miss Filey abruptly stood and left the room.

'Is she OK, do you think?' asked Roo.

'Maybe she's gone to have a lie-down,' said Willard. 'You know, from shock.'

'Look!' said Ed. Attlee, having yawned and stretched, was padding over to the jigsaw box. He turned and gave them an enigmatic look, and then bent his head over the box and seemed to study the contents. Then, faster than the eye could register, his paw flashed out and snagged a piece.

'That's not sky,' said Willard, peering at it. 'It's got tiny writing on it. It says "WELCOME TO CORNWALL".'

'That's from the country lane at the bottom of the

picture,' said Ed. 'That's actually quite impressive. I asked him to give us a sign, and he has.'

'A *road sign*!' said Roo. 'Clever Attlee!'

Attlee dropped the piece and made a series of retching noises before coughing up a large hairball and stalking off.

'I'm going to check on Miss Filey,' said Roo, but before she could stand up, Miss Filey came back into the room. She didn't look at all shocked – in fact, she looked as if she'd just been bouncing on a trampoline: quite red in the face, half laughing, her hair sticking out on one side.

'Found it!' she said, holding up a thimble. 'Attlee was quite correct. It was under the fridge, right at the back, I had to use the handle of the ladle to get at it! Thank you, Attlee – do you want one of your cat treats?'

The cat ignored the small and smelly biscuit that she held out to him, so she dropped it on the little table and sat down beside Willard on the sofa. 'Crikey,' she said, 'what an exciting morning!'

'So . . . you really believe what just happened?' asked Ed cautiously. 'You really believe we talked to Attlee, and you don't think it was a dream or a hallucination or CGI or anything?'

'CGI?' asked Miss Filey.

'It's a sort of cake,' said Willard. 'Just kidding.'

Miss Filey gave a puzzled smile. 'How could I not believe it, when it definitely took place?'

'Right,' said Ed, slightly startled. He tried to imagine how his parents would react to an encounter with a talking cat. Hours and hours of puzzled discussion probably, and endless theories about *how* or *why*, while the total amazingness of the whole thing got lost under all the analysis. Miss Filey was definitely a grown-up, but her reaction to what had happened was more like Roo's.

'The thing is,' he said, 'we've wished four times on four candles now, and they've all come true, and each wish lasts as long as the candle burns.'

'And what did you wish for?' asked Miss Filey.

'The first one was an accident,' said Roo. 'I just happened to say that I wished you had a dog.'

'Oh, I *see*.'

'And then the first deliberate one was for a tame ant. And then we wished we could fly, but it's not as good as it sounds because we just ended up sitting in an aeroplane for five minutes.'

'An aeroplane!' exclaimed Miss Filey, clasping her hands. 'Oh, that must have been wonderful, even for a short time!'

There was a pause. In the end it was Willard who asked the question. 'Haven't you ever been in an aeroplane, Miss Filey?'

'No. My parents were rather nervous about flying and so we always had coach holidays, or went to the seaside.'

'Oh.'

'I went on a boat once, to the Isle of Wight.'

'Oh.'

There was another pause. The children looked at one another.

'Would you like to go on another boat now?' asked Roo. 'Maybe sail to your own island?'

Miss Filey's eyes widened. 'Could I?' she asked softly. 'Or could I travel into space? Or wriggle through a gap in the rock and discover a cavern full of lost paintings? I searched through my library last night and found that book again – the one that inspired all my wishes. Any one of them would be marvellous.'

Silently, Roo gave her the matches, and Willard got out the box of candles and pushed one of them into the disgusting little mound of waxy grey chewing gum, and Miss Filey struck a match and said, in a clear voice that trembled a little, 'I wish for one of those wishes that I never had the chance to make.'

And then she disappeared.

CHAPTER 9

Even if you're expecting it, it's not possible to calmly watch a person completely vanish, and all three of them gave a shout of surprise, and Willard scrambled up and stared at the space where Miss Filey had been sitting.

'That's what happened with the dog,' he said, pointing triumphantly. 'You didn't believe me.'

'We do now,' said Ed. 'Remember we'd only just met you. Also, if you keep saying "just kidding" about everything, then people will think you *are*.'

'Thanks, Teach,' said Willard.

Ed shrugged. 'It's called *maturity*,' he said.

'You're not arguing, are you?' asked Roo. The boys didn't answer. Behind them, on the table, the candle burned steadily. 'I hope Miss Filey's having a good time,' said Willard.

The cat walked up to the French windows and stared out. 'I'm going to put Attlee's hairball in the bin,' said Roo. She took the foil wrapper that had contained Willard's chewing gum and used it to pick up the revolting plug of matted hair. The bin was in the kitchen – it was quite a large one with a heavy metal pedal that flipped the top open, and Roo clanged it open and shut a couple of times, enjoying the noise.

Crossing the hall back to the living room, she paused by Miss Filey's little library; the door was partly open and Roo pushed it wider. Next to the globe on the table was a stack of books. The top one was a hardback, with a picture on the cover.

'Hey!' shouted Roo excitedly, going over to the table. 'Come and look at this!'

The title of the book was *Adventure Stories for Girls* and the cover showed a girl sailing across a bright blue sea in a boat with a red sail. Roo opened it and saw the words 'This book belongs to Rosanna May Filey', written in bright blue ink.

'What's up?' asked Ed, coming into the room, with Willard just behind him.

Roo held up the cover. 'This is Miss Filey's book – it

must be the one she got her ideas from.' She turned a page, and saw a pencilled list.

'What was that noise?' asked Willard suddenly.

'What noise?'

'I thought I heard a noise,' he said.

Ed shook his head. 'I didn't hear anything.' He flipped through the illustrated atlas on the table; there were bookmarks on pages that showed Finland, Madagascar and Lesotho.

'It must be nearly four and a half minutes now,' said Willard, who always felt a bit claustrophobic in a room full of books. 'Miss Filey will be coming back any second.' He turned towards the door, just in time to see Attlee streak across the hall and dive into the kitchen. He frowned, puzzled, and then jerked his head up.

'What's that smell?' he asked. '*WHAT'S THAT SMELL???*'

He was first into the living room, but Roo was only a step or two behind him, and she cannoned into his back as he stopped dead just inside the door. The sofa was on fire, the little table tipped over against it. A sheet of filthy black smoke was already rising from the nylon cover.

Willard looked around wildly. 'We need a blanket or a rug or a . . .'

'Or water, I'll get some water,' said Roo, doubling back and immediately falling over Ed.

'LEMONADE,' shouted Ed, pushing her away. 'GET THE LEMONADE. AND DON'T BREATHE IN ANY OF THE SMOKE!'

Willard dodged round the back of the sofa, grabbed a glass from the tray and, with a panicky sweep of the arm, threw the contents all over Ed.

'The SOFA,' shouted Ed.

'Sorry, sorry, hang on.' Willard picked up the second glass and aimed more carefully. This time, there was a great hiss of steam and the smoke turned white, but a flame still danced across the flowered cushions.

'I've got water,' shouted Roo, from the hall.

She ran in with a jug from which she'd just removed a bunch of tulips, and hastily poured the water all over the sofa. Smoke bloomed up and subsided, the air cleared, and the terrible, acrid smell of burned nylon filled the room. A melted black hole leered at them from the centre of the sofa. The cushions were wet. The floor was wet. Ed was wet.

'How did it happen?' asked Roo.

'I heard a noise,' said Willard. 'And then I saw the cat running across the hall.'

Ed pointed to a tiny, fish-shaped object on the floor.

'That's the treat that Miss Filey brought in. She left it on the table. Attlee must have tried to get it, and then the table tipped and the candle rolled onto the sofa.'

'My mum says that you should always blow out a candle before you leave the room,' said Willard. 'I've just remembered that now.'

'I shouldn't have called you to come and see the library,' said Roo, feeling horribly guilty.

Ed shook his head. 'We shouldn't have both left the room. I mean, what's Miss Filey going to say when she sees this mess?'

There was a pause.

'Where *is* Miss Filey?' asked Willard.

Ed looked at his watch. It was, he realized with a shock, nearly ten minutes since Miss Filey had disappeared. Wordlessly, he watched another minute go by.

'I think we have a problem,' he said quietly. For once, there was no sarcasm in his tone. 'Something's gone terribly wrong.'

'But can't we just light another candle and wish Miss Filey was back here?' asked Roo. She looked around. 'Where *are* the candles?'

'They were in the tin box,' said Willard. 'On the little table. And I closed the lid. I'm sure I closed the lid,

I'm almost certain I closed the lid. Actually, I'm totally certain. I definitely closed the lid. Definitely, definitely.' He scanned the carpet around the overturned table. Roo looked behind the sofa and shook her head.

'It has to be here somewhere,' said Ed, his voice breathy with tension. 'What about . . .' He went over to the sofa and inspected the melted black hole at its centre. And then he carefully inserted a hand and drew out a square, warm, soot-encrusted object.

'See,' said Willard, with relief. 'I *knew* I'd closed it.'

It took Ed a while to open the box. He had to keep turning the tin and slowly, slowly easing up the lid, exposing a line of bright metal a millimetre at a time, his hands filthy, black smears all over his sleeves, and then, at last, with a final scrape and a creak, it opened.

All three of them leaned in to look.

All three of them gasped.

There were no longer five unburned candles in the box. Instead, there was a warm white puddle of silver-streaked wax, in which all the wicks lay tangled like a nest of snakes.

Ed looked up at the horrified faces of the other two.

'*Before* this we had a problem,' he said. 'Now we have a catastrophe.'

CHAPTER 10

'What are we going to do?' asked Roo. 'Ed? What are we going to do?'

She looked at him anxiously. Ed always had a plan but now he was silent and frowning. And also quite wet.

'I'll go and get you a towel,' said Roo. 'I forgot you were covered in lemonade.'

Willard stood staring at the contents of the tin box. 'It's basically a big, flat candle, isn't it?' he said. 'Five whole candles stuck together. Maybe if we light it, we'd just get an extra-long wish. In fact, it'd be five times four-and-a-half minutes long which would add up to' – he thought very hard – 'quite a lot of minutes.

We could get tons done in that time. Or like your sister said, we could just wish Miss Filey was back here. Couldn't we? Couldn't we? Ed? Hey, Ed? Why aren't you saying anything?'

'He's thinking,' said Roo, returning with the towel. 'Ed's a very deep thinker.'

'*I* think about things too,' said Willard. 'I just talk at the same time.'

Ed dried his neck and the front of his sweatshirt, and then handed the towel back to Roo.

'*Thank you*,' said Willard.

'What?' Ed blinked up at him.

'She went and got you a towel and you didn't even thank her.'

'I don't mind,' said Roo. 'It's quicker for me than it is for him.'

'But his leg's never going to get better if you keep doing things for him.'

There was a moment of complete silence.

'OK, here's what I'm thinking,' said Ed, ignoring the comment. 'Two things, and they're both really bad. The first is that the wishes only last as long as the candle burns, don't they? So, if we managed somehow to light this great big melted blob and then wished Miss Filey was here, mightn't she just disappear again when it goes out, even if that's longer than usual? And *then* what would we do?'

Willard's eyes widened.

'And the second thing,' continued Ed, 'is that I was reading a book about precious stones last week. Did you know that diamonds are made of *exactly* the same substance as graphite? Graphite's the grey bit in the middle of pencils – the bit that makes a mark on the page. Diamonds and graphite are both made of carbon and the only difference between them, if you looked through an electron microscope, is the way that the carbon atoms are arranged.'

'So?' said Willard.

'So, what if melting these candles is like rearranging atoms – what if it affects everything about them? What if melting them means they're not magic any more? Or what if they're a completely different sort of magic? We wouldn't know until we lit them and made a wish, and then – if it was something bad – it would be too late to stop it.'

Roo shivered; the thought was so chilling that the room actually seemed to grow colder.

And then it definitely grew smellier.

'Attlee,' said Willard, looking around. The cat was peering around the door.

'Poor puss cat,' said Roo. 'I expect he was frightened by the fire.'

'He *caused* the fire,' said Ed.

Attlee padded into the room, sniffing delicately. He glanced at the burned sofa with a look of disgust, and then stalked around it and lay on the floor.

'I wonder what time Miss Filey feeds him?' said Roo.

There was a loud miaow and a scrabbling sound. Attlee had one paw extended under the sofa, as if trying to reach something.

'The thing is,' said Willard, 'what you're saying about pencils and diamonds and that stuff just sounds like an excuse to me – we have to rescue Miss Filey, and I'm not scared of trying, even if you are.'

Roo stepped forward. 'You'd better not be saying Ed's a coward,' she said to Willard fiercely. 'Because he's the bravest person in the world!'

'How is he brave?' asked Willard. 'Just because he's hurt his leg.'

'He hasn't,' said Roo.

'So why's he sitting in a wheelchair?'

'Because he—'

'*I'll* answer that, Roo,' said her brother, in a voice that could have chopped wood. He turned rather coldly to Willard. 'It's none of your business, but I have a condition that means my muscles don't work properly. I used to be able to walk, but now I can't without leaning on things and getting tired.'

'Oh.' Willard looked uncomfortable. 'So why did you tell me you'd hurt your leg?'

'Because people treat me differently if I tell them the truth. They feel sorry for me and embarrassed and they don't know what to say. Like you, right now.'

For a moment, Willard looked indignant, and then, reluctantly, he nodded. 'Yup,' he said, 'you're right. OK, I promise not to treat you any differently. And that means telling you that you shouldn't snap at your sister like that, when she was just sticking up for you.'

There was a long pause while Ed considered this. 'I suppose I did snap,' he said. 'Sorry, Roo.'

'That's OK,' she said, slightly surprised to get an apology. Ed was often quite snappy, and most of the time she managed to ignore it.

'The truth is, I *am* quite scared,' said Ed, 'because if we light this candle, we're going into the unknown. We don't know where Miss Filey's ended up – we don't even know what was on her list of wishes.'

'*I* do,' said Roo unexpectedly. 'It was written on the inside of her book. Hang on—' She sprinted back into the little library and returned with *Adventure Stories for Girls*.

'Look,' she said, flicking through to the pencilled list.

They clustered round. It was written in neat capitals:

INHERIT A ZOO
TRAVEL TO OUTER SPACE IN A ROCKET
UNEXPECTEDLY STAR IN A FILM
SAIL TO A MYSTERY ISLAND
CATCH A MAJOR INTERNATIONAL CRIMINAL
RESCUE PEOPLE FROM AN AVALANCHE
DISCOVER A CAVE FULL OF STONE-AGE PAINTINGS
ESCAPE FROM A CASTLE
DIVE TO AN UNDERSEA WRECK
EVERYWHERE !!!

'I wonder what "Everywhere" means?' said Willard.

There was another scrabbling sound from the sofa and they looked down to see Attlee dragging a small silver and white object from beneath it.

Roo pounced down and unhooked the object from his claw. It was a candle stub – maybe a couple of centimetres long.

'Look!' she said. 'Where did this come from?' And then she peered at it more closely, and saw that there was a squashed crumb and what looked like a smear of icing stuck to the unburned end. 'It's the one that was in Willard's cake!' she said. 'The very first one we used. When the dog burst in, it must have ended up under the sofa, and missed getting swept up with the rest of the crumbs.'

'It's no good to us though, is it?' said Ed. 'Remember, there's only one wish per candle.'

Attlee miaowed again, and gave Roo what felt like a very hard and significant stare. Carefully, she put the candle stub back in the drawer.

'So, anyway,' said Willard. 'Shouldn't we get on and rescue Miss Filey?'

And then the doorbell rang.

CHAPTER 11

'We can't let anyone in,' said Willard. 'They'll ask where Miss Filey is.'

'*And* they'll ask why the entire house stinks of smoke,' added Ed. 'Not to mention the huge black hole in the sofa.'

The doorbell rang again.

'I'll go, shall I?' asked Roo.

'Don't let them in, whoever it is,' said Ed.

Roo went into the hall and opened the front door just a crack. It was her dad. He was holding a large bunch of flowers.

'Hello!' he said cheerfully. 'Having a nice time?'

'Yes.' She stepped quickly onto the doorstep and pulled the door almost closed behind her.

'What are you up to?' he asked, puzzled.

'We're playing something,' she said. 'Hide and seek,' she added, a bit randomly.

'Oh. Well, I need a quick word with Miss Filey.'

'You can't. She's hiding and I haven't found her yet. Can I give her a message?'

'Where's Ed?'

'He's hiding too. And so's Willard. What's the matter?'

Because she recognized her father's expression – the slightly fixed smile that meant he had something difficult to say. He spoke hesitantly.

'Um . . . the thing is, I was going to thank Miss Filey, and give her these flowers and tell her that this is the last day she'll need to look after you.'

'Why?'

'Well . . .' Her father's smile grew even more fixed.

'*What?*' asked Roo, getting anxious.

'The builders have hit a bit of a problem. They've discovered there's an old well under the garden, and it'll need to be filled in or pumped out before they can start on the extension, which will take more time, and be more expensive, and we really can't afford it at the moment, so they'll have to stop working for the time being until we can find some more money. They're putting up a temporary wall so we can use the living room again.' He was trying to make his voice sound positive and optimistic, but he wasn't really succeeding.

The door behind Roo opened again, and she turned to see Ed. She could tell from his face that he'd been listening.

'You're kidding,' said Ed.

Their father shook his head. 'I'm not, I'm afraid. But we'll sort something out, don't you worry. We'll get your new bedroom built.'

Ed remained silent. More fundraising, he thought. More cupcake sales, and auctions and pictures in the local paper. More people giving him the thumbs up when they saw him in the street, or shouting, 'Hope the 50p I donated really helped!'

'Ed,' said his dad more gently. 'I'm terribly sorry.'

Ed's lips felt like bits of wood. 'Not your fault,' he muttered, turning and starting to go back down the hall.

Their dad took a step forward, as if to follow, and then paused, frowning. 'What's that smell?'

'I'll take the flowers, shall I?' asked Roo quickly. 'I'll give them to Miss Filey.'

'Hang on,' said her dad. 'Is there something burning in the house?'

'No.'

'I'm *sure* I can smell smoke.'

'No, it's just' – Roo thought frantically – 'toast.'

'YES, I WAS MAKING TOAST,' shouted Willard, who'd been listening from behind the living-room door. 'I PUT IT ON THE WRONG SETTING. IT'S NOTHING SERIOUS, IT'S NOT LIKE THE SOFA WENT ON FIRE OR ANYTHING.'

'I'll take these, then,' said Roo, easing the bouquet out of her dad's hand and closing the door. 'Bye!'

There was a pause, and then the letter box opened and her father peered through.

'Are you *sure* everything's all right?' he asked.

'Yup!' said Roo, summoning up a cheery grin. 'No problem, see you later.'

The letter box closed again.

'*I don't think he believed us,*' said Willard, in a very loud whisper.

'Nor me,' said Roo.

Ed said nothing, but his thoughts were clear and precise. Until five minutes ago, the rescue of Miss Filey had seemed to him complex and terrifying and impossible. Now, it was still all those things – but it was also exciting. *Here* meant the dreary muddle of the failed building plans; *there* meant adventure, thrills, the unknown (though it was still, of course, potentially dangerous). He looked at the others.

'Sorry about the building thing,' said Willard, but Ed was already shaking his head.

'I don't want to talk about it,' he said. 'I think we should just get straight on with the rescue. But maybe we shouldn't all go, just in case it's not safe – after all, we've got no idea where we'll end up. Roo, I think you should stay behind.'

'No,' said Roo.

'Listen, I don't often mention that I'm the oldest by a year and a half, but I'm telling you, Roo, that—'

'*No*,' said Roo quietly but firmly, standing with her legs slightly apart and her arms folded. There was zero chance she was going to let Ed go anywhere without her. And though she'd never say it to him – not in a million, billion years – he might *need* her.

'Do you think it *will* be dangerous?' asked Willard.

'It might be,' said Ed. 'We don't know, do we? Would you rather stay here?'

'No *way*. It's just that I . . .' Willard shifted from one foot to another, looking uncomfortable.

'The loo's down the corridor,' said Roo kindly.

'No, it's not that, it's only that I want to' – Willard looked down – 'see my mum,' he said, in a small voice.

'Just for a moment. Before we go. She's helping at a pensioners' lunch just round the corner. I can say hello and I can say' – he took a sharp breath – '*goodbye*, and then I'll come straight back, and I won't mention anything to her about . . . anything. Is that OK?'

The second that Ed and Roo nodded, he was off, closing the front door and running along the quiet street, past the allotments and towards the community centre. The main hall was full of grey-haired people eating apple crumble with custard while a man played a banjo, quite badly.

Willard found his mother in the kitchen, looking harassed in front of a sink full of crockery.

'What's happened?' she asked, turning off the tap. 'Is anything the matter?'

'No, nothing,' said Willard. 'Everything's fine. I was a bit bored. Thought I'd jog round the block and see you.'

'In that case, you can give me a hand. The dishwasher's broken.'

'Oh.'

He'd sort of imagined giving his mum an unexpected hug, and her waving and smiling as he went off again. Instead, he found himself drying about three hundred plates.

'Actually,' said his mum, whose mood had improved since he'd started helping, 'I meant to tell you something funny.'

The things that his mother regarded as funny never seemed to be the same as the things that made Willard laugh, but he put on an interested expression.

'I had a call from the Savings Bank,' she said. 'The one where you've got an account.' It had been set up by Willard's grandmother a few years before and she put in ten pounds every birthday. It now contained forty pounds. 'The bank said that there had been some kind of computer error,' continued his mother, 'and you won't believe it, but for twenty-eight and a half seconds yesterday afternoon, it contained . . . can you guess?'

He was about to shrug when something incredible occurred to him.

'Was it a lot?' he asked tentatively.

'Yes.'

'Was it . . . was it a *million pounds*?'

She laughed with amazement. 'Yes – that was a superb guess! You were a millionaire for less than a minute, and then it all disappeared again. Hang on – where are you off to?'

'I've gotta go!' he said. 'Bye.' He was almost out of

the door when he realized what he'd forgotten to do, and he rushed back and gave his mother a hug before haring back to Miss Filey's house.

CHAPTER 12

'YOU WILL NOT BELIEVE THIS,' Willard was shouting, as he came up the path, and he shouted it again as Roo opened the door, and again in the living room, where Ed was writing something on a piece of paper.

'What won't we believe?' asked Ed.

'Do you remember the tame ant?'

Ed nodded.

'Do you remember when you blew out the candle and the ant disappeared? And there was only a very small bit of the candle left, and I lit it again and had another wish – do you remember what I wished for?'

'A million pounds,' said Ed. 'But nothing happened.'

'But it DID!' shouted Willard, waving his arms. 'My mum's just told me that for twenty-eight seconds yesterday there was a million pounds in my savings account. The bank thought it was a computer error, but it wasn't – it was the wish! For twenty-eight seconds I WAS A MILLIONAIRE! If I'd known, I could've bought a . . . a . . . gold CAR or something. Though I can't drive. Maybe a gold bike, then. Or a skateboard – a platinum skateboard with my name in diamonds, or a—'

He realized that Ed was leaning forward, eyes wide.

'What's the matter?' he asked Willard.

'So that tiny little bit of candle gave you a second wish?'

'Yes.'

'But that means—'

Roo gasped, and dashed to the drawer, and took out the little wax stub that Attlee had found under the sofa. 'It means we've got an extra wish!' she said. 'Though only a small one.'

'But it might get us out of trouble,' said Ed.

'And it's thanks to me,' said Willard, keen to get a bit of credit. 'I had the idea of making a second wish.'

'You and Attlee,' said Ed.

Roo put the leftover candle on a paper napkin and folded it into a tight little package which she stuck in the arm-pocket of Ed's wheelchair. Also in the pocket were a packet of sandwiches, a bottle of water, a pencil and Miss Filey's book, with the list of wishes written in it.

'What if the wheelchair gets left behind?' asked Willard.

'It's not going to be,' said Ed, in a steely voice.

'You didn't have it on the aeroplane.'

'That's because the wish we made was very vague and non-specific. This time it's going to be *exact*.' He showed Willard the bit of paper he was holding.

On it were the words:

We wish that all of us, including Ed and his wheelchair can go straight to where Miss Filey went.

'OK, well, let's get on with it then,' said Willard. 'And fortunately I'm wearing my lucky T-shirt.' He lifted his jumper to show a grey top with a large arrow and the words 'I'M WITH THIS IDIOT' on it. The arrow was pointing towards Ed.

'How has it been lucky?' asked Ed.

'It hasn't. I only got it for my birthday, but it hasn't been *unlucky* yet.'

Ed smoothed out the piece of paper. 'OK. Are we all ready?' he asked.

The other two nodded. Roo was very pale.

'Are you sure, Roo?' asked Ed. 'After all, we're going into the unknown.'

'I'm sure,' she said, taking a match from the box. Her voice was quiet but firm.

The tin of molten candles had been placed in a large saucepan, for safety, and for extra safety the saucepan had been put on a metal tea tray. Ed had used the tip of a knife to gently tease out the ends of the five wicks from the surrounding wax, until enough was sticking out to actually light. The sinuous lines of the wicks looked like waterweed in a frozen pond, the stems sometimes clustered, sometimes separated.

'Strike the match, Roo,' said Ed.

Her hand trembled slightly, but it lit first time.

'I'll count three, two, one,' said Ed, 'and when I get to "one" you hold the match to the candle wicks, and we all read the wish together, OK?'

'Can I be the one who says three, two, one?' asked Willard.

'I suppose so,' said Ed, 'if you want.'

'Only you're doing everything.'

'It's not a *competition*.'

'Yes, but it's like you're in charge, or something.'

'Quickly, it's going to burn my fingers,' said Roo.

'Three-two-one,' said Willard, very fast.

Roo jerked the match towards the wicks, and they all spoke at once but at different speeds, in a jumble of voices:

'WE ALL WISH THAT—'

'INCLUDING ED'S WHEELCHAIR—'

'TO WHERE MISS FILEY WENT—'

The five wicks flared brightly.

And they were no longer in Miss Filey's living room.

They were in her kitchen, instead.

'Whaaaat?' said Willard, gazing open-mouthed at the sink and the neatly folded dish towel and the flowered roller blind that covered the window. 'I thought we'd be . . . you know . . . in a jungle or something.'

'Or on a desert island,' added Roo. She looked around the large, tidy room, lined with green-painted cupboards. A fishy smell hung in the air. 'Where's the bin?' she asked suddenly.

Ed shook his head. A low, flat feeling of disaster was pressing down on him; clearly a great big blob of wax was *not* the same as a separate bunch of candles. 'Who cares about the bin?' he said. 'It's all gone wrong, hasn't it?'

'But there was a bin here about an hour ago and it's gone. It's where I put the hairball that Attlee sicked up.'

'I did not *sick* it *up*,' said Attlee, walking out from under Ed's wheelchair. 'I deliberately *regurgitated* it. It's a high-level skill that humans don't possess.'

'How come you can talk again?' asked Ed.

'Because we're in another one of those tiresome wishes, and you were kind enough to include the phrase "all of us" while I was in the vicinity. There's nothing I wanted more than to be removed from a warm living room where I was having a peaceful nap behind the remains of a once-comfortable sofa and enrolled in some kind of half-baked interdimensional junior rescue mission.'

'But we haven't gone anywhere,' said Willard. 'Only from the telly room to the kitchen.'

'Of course we've gone somewhere,' said Attlee. 'What can you smell?'

There was a pause.

'Well, *you*, obviously,' said Ed.

Attlee's eyes narrowed. 'Anything else?' he asked. 'Any other odour you might have expected?'

'Oh,' said Roo. 'I can't smell the sofa any more. Why's that?'

'Because this isn't the same house.'

Ed frowned. 'Yes, it is.'

'It's not *exactly* the same,' said Roo hesitantly; she wasn't used to contradicting Ed. 'As well as the bin being missing, the fridge is different – it's more old-fashioned – and the taps aren't the same and—'

The door slammed shut.

'Who did that?' asked Ed.

'The floor's fizzing,' said Willard.

They all looked down. The red-tiled surface looked perfectly normal, but they could all feel it vibrating, as if there was a drill in the next room.

'What's happening?' asked Roo.

Abruptly, the vibration increased. The table started shuddering across the floor, and from the kitchen cupboards came the sound of rattling crockery. On the wall, a row of metal kitchen implements, hanging on hooks, began to swing in jangling unison.

'This is weird,' said Willard. The whole kitchen began to shake, the roller blind swaying as if blown by a strong wind, sending light and shadow flickering across the walls. 'Is it an earthquake?' But as he spoke, he felt another sensation – one that was so familiar, and yet so completely *wrong*, that it took him a moment to work out exactly what it was.

'We're going UP!' he shouted, with disbelief.

CHAPTER 13

'We can't be going up,' said Ed, but he knew that they were – knew from the plunging sensation in his stomach, and the feeling that he was being pinned to his chair. They were rising and they were rising *fast*, as if they were in an express lift, except that he'd never heard an express lift make the extraordinary rolling, rumbling sound that he could hear all around them. Roo and Willard were standing with their backs pressed to the cupboards, their eyes wide, their hands gripping the work surfaces, while Attlee lay flattened on the floor, all four legs outstretched. Over the rumbling noise, Ed could just hear the words '. . . you'll find I shall be putting in a strongly worded complaint to the Cats Protection League . . .'

The light spilling into the room from around the swaying roller blind seemed to be getting stronger and brighter with every second.

'Willard,' shouted Ed. 'Can you reach the blind?'

'What?' asked Willard, his teeth clenched to stop them rattling.

'You're nearest the window. Can you reach the blind and see what's outside?'

'OK.' The room was shaking so much that Willard felt as if he was on a fairground ride. He took a couple of tentative steps and then lunged forward, aiming at the cord, but instead getting a handful of flowered material. He gave it a yank and the whole blind fell off, and outside, where there should have been a view of the garden and the garden wall and the back of his own house, was nothing but a dazzlingly blue sky.

'What's going on?' he shouted.

'Don't you remember?' said Ed, with sudden certainty. 'Don't you remember that one of Miss Filey's wishes was to travel into outer space? We're in a rocket.'

'But it's not a proper rocket,' said Willard. 'How can we go into space in a *kitchen*?'

'Look!' shouted Roo.

'I'm looking,' muttered Ed, and the light was so bright that he had to shade his eyes with a hand.

'No,' said Roo, 'look at the walls. Look at the sink. Look at the cupboards. They've all changed.'

Ed dragged his gaze from the window, and for a moment couldn't understand what he was seeing; it was the same and yet not the same. The draining board was still polished metal, but now it was covered with blinking lights and rows of switches. Each of the cupboard doors had acquired a chrome edge and a screen at its centre, showing figures and wavy lines. The fridge had sprouted a keyboard. Dials and diagrams dotted the walls. The row of large spoons and ladles and potato mashers, all hanging from hooks, were now a set of oddly-shaped metal levers.

'Miss Filey said that she used to imagine the wishes happening in the house,' said Roo. 'I think we're in her wish!'

'I wonder what these do,' said Willard, peering at the row of levers.

Ed dragged his attention back to the window. The blue seemed to be deepening and darkening, and now he could see tiny dots of brighter light scattered across the sky. No – not dots, *stars*. And the vibration seemed to be lessening, which meant . . .

'We're leaving the atmosphere,' he shouted,

reaching out to grab a cupboard handle. 'You'd better hold onto something.'

'Why?' asked Willard.

'Because soon we'll be out of earth's gravitational field, and . . .' All at once, the vibration stopped; the window filled with stars and Ed's stomach seemed to unclip itself from his insides and perform a slow somersault.

'Oh, for heaven's sake, what *now*?' asked Attlee, floating upwards, like a badly hoovered magic carpet. 'This is utterly outrageous.'

'I'm flying!' said Willard, sliding sideways through the air towards the sink. 'The table's flying. Everything's flying!'

Ed held onto the cupboard and fended off a tea towel, which had drifted into his face. Just in front of him, his wheelchair was hanging upside down, the contents of the arm-pocket spreading around it, like moons orbiting a planet.

'Are you all right, Ed?' called Roo, from somewhere above him, except that Ed could no longer sense an 'up' or a 'down' – he could see his hand gripping the cupboard handle, but he wasn't sure if he was dangling from a ceiling or performing a one-armed handstand on a floor. He let go, and seemed to hang, motionless, like a speck of dust in a sunlit room, except that this room was slowly rotating around him. It gave him the same feeling as being on the waltzer at the fair. Roo, hanging onto the lampshade with one hand, could see his face turning a greenish-grey.

'Are you all right, Ed?' she called for a second time.

'Space sickness,' he said, closing his eyes and grabbing the cupboard handle again. He reached out his other hand and gripped the wheelchair.

'If this is a wish, then it has to end soon, doesn't it?' asked Roo.

'Hope not,' said Willard cheerfully, kicking off from the wall and diving across the full width of the room towards the stove, pushing the floating table aside as he did so. A frying pan moved past him like a slow-motion Frisbee.

'Ow,' said Attlee, colliding with one of the table legs and going into a slow spin. 'Ow,' he said again, bumping into another. 'Honestly, don't give me a thought,' he said, drifting past Roo. 'I can see you're all frightfully busy. Do please continue to gaze slack-jawed at the view as I helplessly ricochet between every single item in the room.'

Roo scooped him out of the air and guided him into the narrow gap between the top of the cupboards and the ceiling. 'If you hunch up, you should be able to wedge yourself in there,' she said.

Attlee wriggled around until he was safely fixed. 'You're possibly more intelligent than you look,' he said to Roo. 'Watch out, incidentally,' he added, looking over her shoulder.

Roo turned to see a book heading towards her face, and as she pushed it aside she saw that it was the copy of *Adventure Stories for Girls* that she'd tucked into the pocket of Ed's wheelchair. The pages were fanned out like a peacock's tail, and she glimpsed a list of the story titles, and an illustration of a girl in school uniform peering at the moon through a window. Behind the book floated all the other items they'd brought with them.

'Do you want some water, Ed?' asked Willard, casually catching the bottle as he zoomed past on another cross-room dive.

'No,' said Ed, opening his eyes to see that Willard had already pushed himself off from the ceiling and was heading at speed towards the cupboards.

'I'm getting quite good at this,' said Willard, braking at the last second by grabbing onto the row of metal levers. The one that looked like a bit like a potato masher swung downwards with a loud clunk. A light went on just above it. A beeper sounded, then another, and then a loud, shrill bell rang twice.

'What's happening?' asked Ed.

The bell rang for a third time.

And the gravity came back on.

CHAPTER 14

Everything hit the floor, starting with Ed, who was nearest to it, followed by the wheelchair.

The table landed at an angle, snapping off two legs, the water bottle landed squarely on the sandwiches, sending half a tomato skidding across the floor like an ice-hockey puck, and Roo landed on Willard – which was lucky really, because she'd had the furthest to fall. As it was, her head smacked against his knee, while Willard got one of her elbows in his stomach and lay gasping like a fish on land.

'Ow,' said Roo, sitting up, holding her head. She could feel an egg of a bruise pushing against her fingers. 'Are you all right, Ed?' she asked.

He sat up, already feeling better, and checked that the wheelchair was undamaged before pulling himself back into it. 'Yes. What about you two?'

'I'm OK. You OK, Willard?' asked Roo. 'Sorry about the elbow.'

Willard attempted to speak, gave up and raised a thumb in the air. For a moment they all sat wordlessly, only Willard's harsh breathing breaking the silence.

'In case anyone is in the slightest bit interested, I am entirely unhurt,' came a voice from above the cupboards.

'I don't understand,' said Ed. 'How could that lever have turned the gravity back on? That's not possible. That's not . . . *scientific*.'

'Is *any* of it scientific?' asked Willard.

'Yes. I mean, I know we're in a flying kitchen, but what we were seeing out of the window looked right, and the weightlessness was right, and then Willard yanks on a potato masher and suddenly we're all sitting on the floor. It's mad. There don't seem to be any *rules*.'

Willard hauled himself to his feet and looked around, peering at the row of levers. 'We could turn the gravity back off again,' he suggested hopefully.

'No,' said Ed, Roo and Attlee simultaneously.

Willard let out a sigh and wandered over to the window. 'I can see the moon,' he said. 'It's huge. And there's a big thing right in front of it, with a sort of tail.'

'Let's have a look,' said Ed, joining him at the window. Silhouetted against the white disc of the moon was a reddish object shaped a bit like a tadpole, the body round and the tail streaming out in long, dark strands.

'It's a comet,' said Ed. 'Except . . .' He stared at it for a moment, frowning, '. . . it's not really. It's what people imagine comets look like – if you see real photos they're more sort of icy smears. It's like a *drawing* of a comet.'

'You mean it's like this?' asked Roo. She'd been collecting up all the bits that must have fallen out of the wheelchair pocket: the wrapped candle-stub, the water bottle, the matches, a folded-up piece of lined paper – and now she appeared beside Ed, holding *Adventure Stories for Girls*, which she'd found splayed-open in a corner, its spine cracked and the pages loose. She showed him the illustration she'd seen when it had floated past her.

'Yes,' said Ed. 'Exactly like that. *Exactly*.'

Underneath the drawing of the girl was a caption:

Veronica stared at the comet. 'It's getting nearer!' she exclaimed.

'That comet's getting nearer,' said Willard, still looking out of the window. Ed and Roo glanced at each other, eyes wide.

'Look at this, Willard,' said Ed, holding out the picture.

Willard looked at it and gaped.

Ed started flicking back through the book. 'It's from a story called "Veronica Saves the Ship".' He quickly scanned the opening lines. 'Listen to this,' he said.

'I have a surprise for you, Veronica,' said Miss Beale, the headmistress of Fenchurch Hill School for Girls. 'Usually, the winner of the Lower Sixth Mathematics Prize gets a silver cup, but this year I received a letter from the International Space Agency, offering a place on the Jupiter mission to the girl with the greatest talent for numbers.'

'I don't think that would ever happen,' said Willard.

'No,' said Ed. 'It's completely ridiculous, and a journey to Jupiter would take about six years, but I suppose that's where Miss Filey got the idea for the wish from.' He started paging through the story.

'Where is Miss Filey, anyway?' asked Willard.

'I don't know,' said Roo. 'Though maybe . . .'

'What?'

'Maybe she's in a different wish. Maybe melting the candles muddled everything up, like Ed said.'

'So how do we get out of this one? We've been here ages.'

'Listen to this bit,' said Ed, looking up from the page.

'I'm weightless!' said Veronica in amazement as her feet left the floor.

'Brace yourselves,' barked Captain Price to the crew. 'I'm going to switch on the gravity lever now.'

'And there's another picture,' he added, showing them the illustration of a square-jawed astronaut reaching out towards an instrument panel, while Veronica floated in the background, her school tie sticking out horizontally.

'When I won a prize at my last school,' said Willard, 'all I got was a certificate.'

'What was it for?' asked Roo.

'Trying,' said Willard.

'I've never won anything, but Ed got a trophy last year for his science project, didn't you, Ed? And a book token for maths and another book token for English and a voucher for two free pizzas for cookery.'

'Free pizzas!' said Willard. 'That's incredibubble! Were they stuffed crust?'

'I think we should concentrate on the current situation,' said Ed. 'But no, they weren't, they were thin 'n' crispy. I shared a Hawaiian with Mum, and Dad and Roo had an American Hot.'

'And it was *really* hot,' said Roo. Even remembering it seemed to make her feel hotter. She wiped her forehead. And then Willard wiped his. And then Ed looked around, his face beaded with sweat. 'Hang on,' he said. 'It's getting warmer in here. Much, much warmer.'

'The window's steamed up!' exclaimed Roo. She leaned across the dials and switches that covered the draining board and dragged her sleeve across the glass. The moon was revealed again, but now only the rim of it was visible; the comet, instead of being a small silhouette, had grown huge and dark red, the surface flickering with fire.

'Comets aren't hot,' said Ed.

'This one is,' said Willard.

'They're made of ice.'

'This one isn't.'

And as they stared, the outline of the moon suddenly disappeared and all they could see against the star-filled sky was the comet, coming towards them. Fast.

CHAPTER 15

'I don't think I like this wish,' said Roo, her eyes still fixed on the comet.

'Don't worry,' said Ed, trying to sound grown-up and reassuring. 'We'll be fine, we just need to think really, really hard and we mustn't panic. And we *definitely* mustn't go around randomly touching stuff,' he added hurriedly in Willard's direction.

Reluctantly, Willard withdrew his hand from the ladle-shaped lever next to the potato masher. 'I thought it might be a sort of gearstick,' he said. 'After all, we've got to brake or change direction somehow, haven't we? And there's nothing here that looks like a steering wheel. Hey, look at this!' He pointed at what had once been the fridge. 'It's got a sort of diagram on it.' Most of the top half of the fridge door was a now a screen, and beneath it was a keyboard. On the screen, a red fiery circle was inching towards a blinking black dot. 'We must be that dot,' he said. 'It looks a bit like a game, doesn't it?'

He glanced round at Ed, but Ed was once again leafing through the copy of *Adventure Stories for Girls*, with Roo peering over his shoulder; unobserved, Willard tried typing 'R' for 'right' on the keyboard. Nothing happened, except that the circle moved even nearer to the dot.

'This is just a wish, isn't it?' he muttered. 'We can't *die* in it, can we?' He thought, fleetingly, of his mum, cleaning the kitchen in the community centre, and then he hunched over the keyboard and typed: PLEASE PLEASE PLEASE TURN RIGHT. The red circle moved relentlessly onward.

'Here!' shouted Ed, jabbing a finger at a page. 'Listen to this!'

'We're in trouble!' exclaimed the captain. 'We need to steer away from the comet, but our coordinates to Jupiter are fixed and can only be changed by an incredibly complex mathematical calculation. And

our calculator broke during take-off. If only we had someone here who was really good at maths.'

Hesitantly, Veronica raised her hand.

'So, you mean instead of finding a steering wheel we have to do *sums*?' asked Willard, horrified.

'Looks like it,' said Ed. He turned the page and carried on reading.

Veronica stared, frowning, at the string of figures. 'I think I can work it out,' she said. 'All I need to do is multiply the square root of a hundred by twenty-six thousand nine hundred and ninety-six and then divide it by seventeen.' She thought, hard. 'Yes, I've got it,' she said, and quickly typed the answer into the computer. With a loud 'whoosh' the ship suddenly veered left, leaving the comet far behind, and the crew cheered with relief.

'Jolly well done, Veronica,' said the captain. 'I was totally against having a schoolgirl on board, but I have to admit that I was completely wrong. You're part of the team now!'

Veronica grinned. 'Jupiter, here we come!' she said.

The End

Ed finished reading, and realized that the other two were looking at him expectantly.

'So what *is* the answer to that sum?' asked Willard. 'You're good at maths, aren't you? You got a cup.'

'Give me a moment,' said Ed. He read the sum again. 'OK. The square root of a hundred is ten, and when you multiply something by ten, you just have to add a nought on the end, so twenty-six thousand nine hundred and ninety-six times ten is . . . is . . . two hundred and sixty nine thousand, nine hundred and sixty. So now all I have to do now is divide that number by seventeen.'

There was a long pause.

'Go on then,' said Willard.

'He's *thinking*,' said Roo loyally.

The numbers churned in Ed's head, refusing to stand still or line up. A drop of sweat plopped from his chin onto the page of the book, a page that now seemed to have darkened. The light coming in through the window had changed, and was steeping the whole room in a dull, reddish colour.

'Hello, people,' called Attlee, from the top of the cupboard. 'I don't know if anyone's noticed, but we seem to be heading directly for a gigantic ball of flame.'

'Yes, hurry *up*,' said Willard, jigging up and down with impatience. 'We're going to smash right into it.'

Ed screwed up his eyes and tried to concentrate. 'I know I could do it if I had a pen and paper,' he said.

'I've got paper here,' said Roo, unfolding the piece she'd found on the floor, 'but I don't know if there's a pencil or— OH!' Her eyes wide, she unfolded the paper completely and then turned it round to show Ed and Willard. It was a page ripped out of a small notebook, and on it was a sum, written in pencil:

$$269,960 \div 17 = 15,880$$

'Who did that?' asked Ed. From the corner of his eye he could see the comet almost filling the window. 'No – never mind. It looks right, let's use it.'

'Read it out to me!' shouted Willard, leaping back towards the keyboard.

In a clear voice that shook just a little, Roo recited the numbers and Willard tapped them in. The keys were actually warm, and the air in the room seemed, by the second, to grow thicker and harder to breathe.

'*One . . . five . . . eight . . . eight . . . zero . . .*'

'And ENTER,' said Willard, hammering the 'return'

button. Instantly, the whole room tilted violently, sending the three of them piling into a corner.

'Oh, can I not be allowed to relax for a single *second*,' said Attlee, who had slid off the top of the cupboard and was clinging on by a single outstretched paw, his body dangling like a pendulum. 'Was I asked if I wanted to come? Did anyone bother to consult the most senior member of the party? No, I was simply hurled into – *urk!*'

The room tilted in the other direction, throwing him onto the cupboard again, and sending Roo, Willard and Ed sliding back across the floor.

'Look!' shouted Willard, pointing to the window. The comet was half the size it had been before, and now they were sweeping in a great curve past the pale, pitted disc of the moon.

'Look,' repeated Roo, more softly. The room was reassembling itself, the screens fading from the cupboards, the lights and dials sinking back into the draining board, the brightness of chrome and plastic dulling into wood and tile. The floor straightened up, a cloud seemed to sweep across the window and when it cleared, the back of Willard's house was visible again, across the shrubs and lawn of Miss Filey's garden.

CHAPTER 16

'We're back to normal! Result!' said Willard, high-fiving Roo. 'Team effort,' he added, giving a thumbs up to Ed. 'Total success. Apart from breaking the table and not finding Miss Filey, obviously. Unless she's back in the living room, phoning the fire brigade.'

'Shall I go and check?' asked Roo. 'Are you OK, Ed?' she added; he was being very quiet.

He nodded. 'I'm all right. You go and look for Miss Filey.' He leaned over and picked up the piece of paper that Roo had dropped, the one on which the answer to the sum was written – the answer that he hadn't been able to work out in his head, despite having won a prize for maths.

'I'll go too,' said Willard, turning to follow Roo.

From the top of the cupboards came the sound of a noisy throat clear. 'So, I'll just stay up here, shall I? Goodbye, then. Have a simply marvellous life.'

'Sorry,' said Willard. 'I thought . . . you know . . . cats jump, don't they?'

'Oh, you want me to *jump*?' Attlee peered over the edge. 'Yes, that seems a characteristically thoughtful suggestion, given that in human years, I'm approaching the age of a hundred and twenty-five. I'll count to three, shall I, and then *launch* myself into a world of multiple fractures? *One* . . .'

'OK, OK,' said Willard, clambering onto the draining board. 'How come you can still talk, anyway?'

Attlee rolled his eyes. 'Because, clearly, we are not *in any way* "back to normal". While you're up here, incidentally, could you check in the cupboard for Fishee Treats? They should be on the top shelf. No?'

'Nope,' said Willard.

'Chicken Nibbles?'

'Nope.'

'Rabbit-Flavoured Delites for the Senior Puss in Your Life?'

'No cat food at all,' said Willard.

'Miss Filey's not in the living room,' reported Roo,

returning, breathless, 'but everything's different. The sofa's not burned and there's no telly, only a huge radio. I'm going to have a look in the other rooms, just in case she's there.'

'Fine,' said Ed continuing to stare at the carefully written numbers on the paper.

'Thank you,' said Attlee icily, as Willard lowered him to the floor. 'Incidentally, is anyone going to wipe up the remains of that tomato, or do something about the state of the paintwork? Or is your aim to systematically trash every room while your hostess is absent?'

'Oh . . .' Ed looked around at the broken table, the squashed sandwich, the tomato skid-mark, Willard's footmarks on the cupboards, walls and ceiling. 'But we're in the middle of a sort of emergency, aren't we?' Attlee stared at him hard, like a particularly stern teacher, and Ed picked up a tea towel and leaned over to wipe up the tomato, while Willard reluctantly rubbed at one of his footmarks with the sleeve of his sweatshirt.

'Miss Filey's library's not a library any more!' called Roo from the hall. 'It's all changed.'

'Be with you in a minute,' said Ed, conscious of Attlee's stare. The cat watched them for a moment or two as they sponged and wiped, and then stalked off in the direction of the hall.

Ed immediately dropped the cloth and picked up the piece of paper again. He stared at it, frowning.

'Why do you keep looking at that?' asked Willard.

'Because . . . because I'm annoyed with myself.'

'Why?'

'Because I should have been able to do that sum in my head. I should have managed it easily. I put us in danger.'

Willard shrugged. 'It was all right in the end though, wasn't it?'

'Yes, but that's what I'm supposed to be good at. I can't run around, but I'm good at *thinking*.'

'Well, I'm supposed to be good at running around, but that doesn't mean I win all the races. Anyway, I bet the maths prize wasn't for doing some massive sum while heading straight for a comet with people waving their arms and shouting, "HURRY UP OR WE'RE ALL GOING TO DIE!" at you, was it?'

'Well . . . no,' said Ed, smiling rather unwillingly.

'Made you laugh,' said Willard. 'Class clown! Come on, let's go and see what your sister's found.'

The hall looked unchanged, with sunlight shining through the window above the front door and pooling in a fan-shaped pattern on the wooden floor, but through the open living-room door they could see that the sofa looked brand-new, and where the telly had been was a set of bookshelves and a large radio.

'Roo!' called Ed. There was no answer.

Willard opened the door of the dining room. There was a cloth on the table that hadn't been there before, laid with three sets of knives and forks. 'She's not in here,' he said.

'Nor here,' said Ed, peering into the bathroom, where three toothbrushes stood in a pot. 'Roo,' he called again. 'Where's she gone?' He went over to the door of Miss Filey's library and turned the handle. The door stayed shut.

'Is it locked?' asked Willard. 'Shall I have a go?' He jerked the handle up and down a few times, with no result.

'Roo, open the door,' shouted Ed, knocking. 'Are you OK? Roo!'

'It must have been open before,' said Willard, 'because she went in there, didn't she? She called to us about it looking different.' He pressed an ear to the door. 'Can't hear anything,' he said. 'Shall I try and kick it down like they do in films? I did three karate lessons last year and they said I had definite potential if I concentrated more and didn't talk so much.'

Ed hesitated, and then looked around to see if Attlee was watching. There was no sign of him. 'OK,' he said, 'give it a go. I'll move back a bit.'

Willard took a couple of deep breaths, leaned over, lifted one leg and thudded a great kick just below the door handle. 'OW!' he shouted, immediately doubling over and rubbing his knee and shin. 'Ow, Ow, Ow.' The door hadn't even shuddered. 'That didn't feel normal. That was like kicking a boulder.'

'Roo!' called Ed again, feeling frightened now. '*Roo!!*' He hammered on the door with the flat of his hands, and he could feel what Willard had meant; it was as if the room was not just locked but sealed shut, like a cave after a rock fall. 'Why isn't she answering?' he asked. 'What's going on in there? *Where is my sister?*'

CHAPTER 17

Roo was sitting in a chair, drinking a cup of tea, trying to breathe through her mouth, because Attlee was sprawled on her lap. Apart from the smell, she was really enjoying herself. She had never been to a film studio before.

Barely ten minutes ago, she had been tearing round the bungalow, looking for Miss Filey, glancing in every room, each time spotting little indications that this was not quite the same house that she and Ed and Willard had been visiting for the past few days.

Everywhere were signs that three people were living here – three table mats, three toothbrushes, three umbrellas in the hall. Everything looked slightly newer – the colours less faded, the materials less worn – but nothing had changed quite as much as Miss Filey's library.

Roo had opened the door and gasped. Instead of shelves, there was a small bed covered with a knitted blanket, a little desk on which there was a pile of schoolbooks, and a bedside table on which sat a blue teddy bear and a framed photograph.

'Miss Filey's library's not a library any more!' she called over her shoulder, to the boys. 'It's all changed.' And she went into the room and picked up the framed photograph.

It showed three people standing on top of a hill, with a wide view of lakes and mountains behind them: a cheerful, round-faced man, holding his hat on to stop it blowing away, a tall, healthy-looking woman wearing a headscarf and squinting into the wind, and a grinning girl with her plaits blowing sideways; the girl was unmistakably Miss Filey.

'Oh, there you are,' said Attlee, strolling through the open door. 'I don't suppose you have any Fishee Treats on you, do you? I'm beginning to feel rather faint.'

'I'm sorry, I haven't,' said Roo, as Attlee flopped onto the striped rug. 'What's Ed doing? Is he all right?'

'He and Willard are cleaning up the kitchen,' said Attlee casually, as if that was a normal sort of statement.

'*Cleaning up the kitchen?*' repeated Roo, astounded. 'Will he be long?'

'I very much doubt it,' said Attlee. 'I detected a certain lack of enthusiasm.'

'I need to tell him something – I think I know what's happening. I think this house is back the way it was when Miss Filey was a little girl, when she imagined all the wishes happening right here. Though I still don't know where she is. Do you?'

'I'm afraid not,' said Attlee, resting his chin on his paws, and then immediately straightening up. 'I've just realized something,' he said, looking down, his voice trembling.

'What? Something about Miss Filey?'

'No, something about this rug. It used to be next to the back door when I was a kitten, and it was my *favourite* rug!' He flexed his claws a couple of times, and there was a sound of ripping fibres. 'This was the happy rug of my youth. It gave me many hours of innocent joy before, for some inexplicable reason, it was removed from the house and *hurled* into the bin.' He dragged one outstretched paw towards himself, leaving a long trail of loops and broken threads right across the pattern. 'Oh!' he said, eyes half-shut with pleasure. 'That beautiful, beautiful noise!'

'QUIET, PLEASE!' shouted a man, very loudly.

'Who was that?' asked Roo, startled. The bedroom door slammed shut and then the entire wall slid to one side, revealing an enormous indoor space, filled with people and equipment – huge cameras on wheels, a gigantic microphone on a long pole and electrical cables snaking in all directions. A bright light shone from above, and Roo looked up to see that there was no longer a bedroom ceiling, only a studio roof far overhead, criss-crossed with lamps and rails.

'Oh, not *again*,' said Attlee.

'REHEARSAL ABOUT TO START,' shouted the same man.

'Excuse me, dear,' said a smartly dressed woman, holding a clipboard and a stopwatch. 'You need to move away from the set. And did your uncle say that you could bring your pet with you?'

'My uncle?' Roo looked around, bewildered.

'Yes, your uncle, who works in the studio as a caretaker and who arranged for you to come and watch the filming as a birthday treat,' said the woman helpfully, as if reading from a book.

'Oh,' said Roo. 'Yes.' *I'm in a wish*, she thought, *and*

I'm all on my own, apart from Attlee. And she felt both a flutter of fright and an odd sense of freedom, because Ed and Willard were safely cleaning up the kitchen, and for once she only had to worry about herself.

She followed the woman with the clipboard towards a chair. Miss Filey's bedroom, with its little bed, rug and desk, was now a spotlit island to one side of an enormous dark floor. There were other brightly lit sets scattered across the studio: the front door of a house with windows on either side, a car in front of a closed garage door and a set of railings in front of a row of flowering bushes.

'Cup of tea, love?' said a woman with an apron and a trolley full of mugs, and a cigarette sticking out of one side of her mouth. 'How many sugars?'

Roo couldn't ever remember being asked that question before.

'Three, please,' she said experimentally. The woman stirred them into the tea without comment and then opened a tin containing an enormous iced cake with coloured sprinkles. 'Here, love,' she said, 'have a nice slice of this as well.'

'Do you have any Fishee Treats?' asked Attlee, but the trolley was already moving away.

'I think this is another wish from the book,' said

Roo, taking a bite of cake. 'I saw the list of stories at the beginning, and there was one called something about being an unexpected film star.' She felt quite excited; this wasn't like hurtling to danger in a shuddering kitchen, this was more like an enjoyable daydream. She sipped the tea, which was deliciously sweet. 'This must be the olden days,' she said. 'When people smoked all the time, and grown-ups encouraged children to eat lots of sugar.'

'This floor's dreadfully uncomfortable,' said Attlee. 'How I miss my lovely rug!' He looked pointedly at Roo, and she scooped him onto her lap.

'ALL RIGHT, EVERYONE, GET READY TO REHEARSE! DIRECTOR AND STAR ON SET.'

Roo craned to see what was going on. A very pretty girl of about her own age, wearing a hair ribbon and a fussy, frilly dress, was walking across the studio floor, accompanied by a tall, anxious-looking man in a wide-brimmed hat.

'Sorry about the delay, Davina,' he was saying. 'We had a problem with one of the lights. Still, I expect you were busy working with your tutor, weren't you?'

'No, she's ill, so I was sitting in my dressing room with absolutely nothing to do.'

'Oh dear.'

'There's not even a radio in there. On my last film, in Hollywood, whenever there was a long wait I had my own private cinema and a chef who'd cook me anything I wanted. And my very own trailer with a full-sized ping-pong table. And a guinea pig to stroke whenever I got bored.'

'Well, we can't quite afford that here,' said the man, with an attempt at a smile. 'So, if we could just rehearse this scene,' he continued, leading Davina into the little bedroom. 'Your character, Emmeline, who's just been sent to live with her rich aunt and uncle, is sitting on the bed, thinking about her parents, and—'

'I know, I know,' interrupted Davina. 'I know all my words. On my last film, they called me "Little Miss Perfect". I'm going to start by sitting on the bed' – she sat down on it – 'and then I'll look up wistfully' – she looked up wistfully – 'and then I'll say' – her voice dropped to a husky, sorrowful croak – *'I know my mother and father just wanted the best for me, but oh, how I miss them. I miss them so much.'*

'She's good, isn't she?' whispered Roo to Attlee.

Davina turned her head sharply. 'Who's that speaking?' she demanded. Everyone – and there seemed to be about a hundred people in the studio – turned to look at Roo.

'Sorry,' she muttered, her face flaming.

'I need *complete* silence when I'm rehearsing. Also, there's an absolutely *disgusting* smell in here.' She continued to look accusingly at Roo, who hunched forward in an effort to conceal Attlee.

'Shall we carry on?' asked the director hopefully.

Davina stared at Roo for a second longer, and then settled herself on the bed again before continuing. 'So, after I say the line, I'll stand up' – she stood up – 'and then I'll run towards where the door's supposed to be.' She started to run towards where the door was supposed to be, caught her foot on something and fell flat on her face.

'HA!' said Attlee quite loudly.

'Who laughed?' demanded Davina, scrambling to her feet. 'Who laughed at me?'

Roo folded her arms over Attlee.

'I'm sure no one did,' said the director, sounding slightly panicky. 'I think it was just a cough.' He peered at the floor, where Davina had fallen. 'I'm afraid we've been given a damaged rug – you must have caught your foot in that loop of thread. Are you hurt?'

'Yes, I am. *Badly*.'

'Your knees?'

'My feelings,' said Davina dramatically. 'Which

are even more important than my knees. I'm taking the rest of the morning off to recover, and then I'm going to speak to my agent and see if he can tear up my contract. I never wanted to do this stupid film in the first place – I'm not used to cheap sets and constant interruptions, and I'm certainly not used to vile *smells*.' She aimed the last words in Roo's direction, and then walked away across the studio, her footsteps very loud.

There was a moment's silence and then the director sat heavily on the nearest chair, a hand over his eyes. 'What on earth are we going to do if she leaves?' he asked. 'Without the star there's no film, and if there's no film' – he looked up at the crew – 'there's no work. We're finished.'

CHAPTER 18

'How long's she been in there now?' asked Willard, trying the handle of the room for about the twentieth time.

'Nearly ten minutes,' said Ed. 'I've just had a thought. It's about what Roo said – that when Miss Filey was little, she'd imagined all the wishes taking place right here, in her house. Do you remember?'

There was a pause. 'Not really,' said Willard. 'Loads has been happening, hasn't it? It's like going to a theme park and then trying to remember what your mum told you about some shoes she wanted to buy.'

'OK, well, Miss Filey definitely said that she used to stand in the hall and wonder which story to visit.

So, I wonder if that's what the messed-up candles have done – they've sent us back to that time, which is why everything's so old-fashioned. And when Roo went into this room, it turned into a wish!'

He started to leaf through the *Adventure Stories* book. 'We've done the one with the rocket, but there's one about a castle . . . and one about a zoo – a tiger escapes, hope it isn't that one . . . and one about a film studio – there's a picture of a girl looking at a film script and a director or somebody pointing at a camera – hope it's not that one, either.'

'Why?'

'Because Roo can't act. Or she can only act if the part she's playing is exactly like her. Dad says she's too honest. She ended up being cast as a non-speaking tree when the school did *The Three Bears* last year, because she couldn't pretend she liked porridge.'

Willard tried the handle again. 'I've got an idea,' he said. 'Why don't we go outside and round the house and look in through the window?'

Ed stared at him, surprised. 'Why didn't I think of that?' he asked. 'OK, let's do it, but we ought to leave a note for Roo in case she comes out again.' He found a pencil in a drawer in the telephone table, but no paper, and he opened the *Adventure Stories* book with the idea of ripping out one of the blank pages near the front. And stopped. And stared.

'What?' asked Willard.

'The list of wishes. The handwriting.' Ed fished in the side-pocket of his wheelchair for the scrap of paper on which the rocket sum had been written. 'Look,' he said, smoothing it out beside the list.

'I-*dent*-i-ca-bubble,' said Willard dramatically.

'Yup. Miss Filey wrote both. Which means that she was in the rocket wish before we were.'

'On her own!'

'Yes. She must have been scared.'

'*And* she must be really, really good at maths. So, where's she now?'

'I don't know,' said Ed, ignoring the maths remark. 'In another wish, maybe? There were five candles all stuck together, weren't there – so five wishes. Maybe she's in there with Roo. Fingers crossed.'

'And maybe Attlee's there too,' said Willard. 'I haven't smelled him anywhere.'

'Well, *he* won't be much use,' said Ed. He started carefully to rip out one of the blank pages, and found that it came away in his hand, loosened from the battering the book had taken in the rocket. He wrote:

Dear Roo, please stay in the hall till we get back. Don't go anywhere else. We won't be long, Ed. xxxx and Willard.

He placed the page in the middle of the hall carpet.

'OK,' he said. 'Let's go!'

Willard opened the front door, and then closed it again.

'What's the matter?' asked Ed.

'It's all changed.'

'Changed how? Let's see.'

Willard opened the door again, and they both looked out. The front garden looked the same, and the path, and the gate, but on the opposite side of the street, instead of houses there was a field. A cow was looking over the fence at them.

'This must be before they built the rest of the street,' said Willard.

Ed nodded. 'And do you know what they built *behind* those houses?'

'No.'

'Our school.'

It was weird to see a distant barn and a scattering of sheep where they should have been seeing the entrance to Meadows Primary School.

'What's it like?' asked Willard. 'The school, I mean.'

'It's OK. It's the only one I've ever been to, so I've got nothing to compare it with.'

'This'll be my third,' said Willard. 'The worst bit is when you go into a new class in the middle of the term and they all turn round and stare at you. I don't like that.'

'I'm used to people staring at me,' said Ed. 'You just have to ignore it and pretend you don't care. Come on. Leave the door open – we don't want to get locked out.' They set off down the flagstoned path that wound round the house, past bushes thick with blooms and alongside a small pond, fringed with rushes.

'Frog,' said Willard, pointing.

'It's a toad.'

'How do you know?'

'Lumpier skin, blunter nose, shorter legs.'

'Right,' said Willard. 'And they give you warts if you pick them up.'

'No, that's just a myth.'

'Is it?' Willard sounded doubtful. 'There's another toad,' he said, pointing.

'No, that one's a frog.'

'And what's *that*?'

'What's what?'

'Didn't you see?' Willard pointed to the middle of the pond. 'There was a sort of splash. And a grey thing. Like a dolphin.'

'Well, it definitely won't be a dolphin.'

Immediately, there was another splash. Ed's mouth dropped open. Out of the water came a beaky snout followed by the perfect shining curve of a grey body. And beside it was another. And another. A pod of dolphins was leaping across Miss Filey's small pond. Except that it wasn't a small pond any longer – it was expanding in every direction, it was spreading to the horizon: it was a vast empty ocean and in the middle of it, in a small boat with a red sail, were Ed and Willard.

CHAPTER 19

'Oh great,' said Ed sarcastically. 'Brilliant. So now Roo's in one wish, and we're in another. It was on Miss Filey's list, wasn't it: SAIL TO A MYSTERY ISLAND? Except there's no island.'

Willard looked around, open-mouthed. Sea stretched endlessly on every side. 'I've been on a boat before but I've never not been able to see the edges,' he said. 'I mean, there's literally nothing.'

Another group of dolphins danced past them, and a light breeze ruffled the surface of the water. The red sail flapped and the boat rocked a little.

Ed felt quite safe, his wheelchair wedged neatly between the boat side and the centreboard.

'There aren't any life jackets, are there?' asked Willard, peering under the seats. 'I got a badge for doing a width last year, but it's not my top skill, or anything.'

Wordlessly, Ed reached round for the tiller with one hand and lightly pulled on the rope attached to the sail with the other. The boat stopped rocking and started to move smoothly.

'How do you know how to do that?' asked Willard.

'Kids in wheelchairs are always getting sent on water skills courses,' said Ed. 'And archery. And ping-pong.' He pulled the rope a little tighter and heard the lovely rippling swish of a sailing boat moving through deep water.

'So, where are we going?' asked Willard, trailing a hand over the side, and then thinking of sharks and taking it out again. 'And how do we get back?'

'We got back from outer space by following the story, didn't we? Have a look through the book and see if you can find one that matches what's happening now.'

Willard opened *Adventure Stories for Girls* and turned to the contents page. '*Belinda Solves a Crime. Rhoda and the Underground Mystery. Jean: Junior Zookeeper. Unexpected Film Star. Veronica Saves the Ship* – we've done that. Oh, here we go: *Delia on Mystery Island*. Page seventy-nine.'

'And there's the island!' exclaimed Ed. 'Straight ahead.' It was a tiny, dark, irregular lump on the horizon, like a currant on a blue tablecloth.

'Page . . . seventy-nine . . .' said Willard, thumbing through. 'Some of these pages are quite loose. OK, I'll read it out.'

'No one's used that boat for many, many years,' said the old salt, sitting on the harbourside. 'And certainly not a young lassie like you. Where are you taking it?'

'What's an old salt?' Willard asked.
'A sailor, I think.'
'OK.'

'It was in the boathouse of our holiday home,' said Delia. 'I thought that as it's such a calm day, I'd take it across to explore the island.'

'Gold Shell Island? No, no, don't do that,' said the old man, shaking his silver locks.

'Why's he got silver locks?'
'It means grey hair,' said Ed.

'Tis dangerous over there, 'tis cursed. They say whoever sets foot on the island must either find the treasure or leave his bones there.'

Delia laughed. She didn't believe in superstition. She untied the half-hitch that held the mainstay sheet to the furling post—

'No idea,' interrupted Ed.

. . . and cast off.

'OK, I'll skip through this bit. It's just sailing stuff.' Willard turned a couple of pages. 'Right, there's a picture here of Delia looking at a map of the island. There's an "X" on it.'

'Where did she find the map?' Ed asked.

'It says . . .'

She could hear a piece of paper flapping. She felt around under the for'ard gunwale and drew out a folded sheet of ancient-looking paper.

'Before you ask,' said Ed, 'I don't know what a "for'ard gunwale" is. Just look everywhere.'

As Willard searched the boat, Ed kept his eye on the

island. It looked small but forbidding, the harsh rock softened by nothing more than the odd stunted bush, the vertical cliffs dropping directly into the sea. Gulls speckled the air around it, their cries faintly audible.

'OK, got it!' said Willard triumphantly, straightening up with a yellowed sheet of paper in his hand. In faded ink, it showed an outline of the island, with an 'X' right at the centre. A double line looped from the 'X' to the sea, where two little triangles and a semicircle had been drawn.

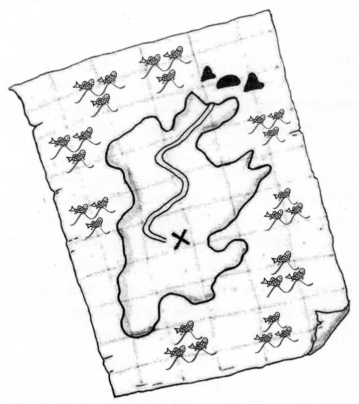

'That looks like a road, doesn't it?' asked Willard, pointing to the double line. 'I suppose it must start at the top of the cliffs, though I don't know how we'd get up there.'

They were much closer now and could hear the smash of the waves around the base of the island. The breeze seemed to be getting stronger and instead of gliding, the boat began to bounce, sending up sheets of spray.

'What does it say next?' asked Ed.

'It says . . .'

Delia frowned at the map. 'How odd,' she said to herself. 'Those lines look like a road, but the island's nothing but barren rock. And what are those shapes at one end of the road? I wonder if—'

Willard turned the page, and a gust of wind caught it, and the page after it as well, and ripped them both out of the book and sent them whirling into the air.

'DON'T STAND UP!' shouted Ed, as Willard stood up. Hastily, he sat down again, gripping the seat as the boat rocked. The pages rose briefly to the height of the mast, and then spiralled gently down again, landing in the sea about a boat-length behind them.

'Can we reverse?' asked Willard, turning to look over his shoulder. 'No, never mind, I think they're starting to sink. Yes, they're definitely sinking. One of them's just sunk, the other's still sinking. Still sinking. Still sinking. Sunk.'

'It wasn't your fault,' muttered Ed, concentrating on his steering.

'I know it wasn't my fault,' said Willard.

'Maybe it was just descriptive stuff. Can you read the next bit?'

Willard lowered the book between his ankles and opened it cautiously. The print was half-obscured by the shadow of his knees, and it took him a while to find the right page. 'Here we go. Oh.'

'What?' asked Ed, frowning ahead. The island was quite near now, and there was nowhere obvious to land: no jetty, no beach, not even a strip of shingle – just a wall of rock, freckled with wheeling gulls.

'It's not great,' said Willard. 'Listen.'

Delia looked back at the narrow mouth of the cave. If it hadn't been for the adventurous seal and the clever clues on the map, she'd never have got past the rocks and found the entrance – the boat might even have been wrecked on their jagged surfaces. She

took out the paddle from the aft starboard gunwale and began to paddle slowly through to the heart of the island.

He flicked ahead. 'She finds some treasure at the end,' he added encouragingly.

Ed heard an odd sound and looked over his shoulder. The horizon was empty, but in the blue middle-distance he could see what looked like a fountain spraying, and then he saw the rolling surge of a vast dark body.

'A whale!' he shouted, and Willard turned just in time to catch the flip of the tail.

'Incredibubble!' said Willard.

'Yup,' said Ed. 'That really was incredibubble.' The sea was an unbroken blue again, the horizon a single straight line. 'What would happen if we didn't follow the story?' he asked. 'Would we sail for ever?'

'I wouldn't want that,' said Willard. 'I'd miss my mum.'

Ed looked towards the island again. He moved the tiller and loosened the sail a little, turning the boat so that it began to follow the line of the shore. Maybe there'd be somewhere to land around the other side.

'Keep a lookout for an adventurous seal,' he said to Willard. 'It shouldn't be too hard to spot.'

CHAPTER 20

In the studio, the director was standing beside the woman with the stopwatch, and they were having a quiet, intense discussion while the rest of the film crew stood around smoking cigarettes and looking extremely worried.

Roo sat with Attlee on her lap and picked at the cake.

'I gather that you're not talking to me,' said Attlee.

'You shouldn't have laughed,' said Roo. 'It must have felt horrible for that girl Davina to fall over in front of everybody.'

'Yes, but she's absolutely ghastly,' said Attlee. 'And I'm a cat. The same rules don't apply to cats.' He yawned and inspected his claws. 'And I'm terribly, terribly hungry.'

'Do you want some cake?'

'Cake?' repeated Attlee, outraged. 'You must be confusing me with a *dog*. I require something savoury. My energy level is plummeting like a headless mouse accidentally knocked off a kitchen table.'

Roo stopped eating.

'All right, everybody, gather round,' said the director. 'We still don't know whether our young star is going to continue, but we have to keep working otherwise we'll fall behind schedule. So, we're going to move on to a short scene that doesn't feature her: page eighty-three of your scripts. A neighbouring mother and daughter watch as Emmeline, the heroine, is thrown out of the house by her rich aunt and uncle after being wrongly accused of stealing. The only problem is that we were going to shoot it tomorrow, and the child playing the daughter isn't in the studio today. However' – he turned to the woman with the stopwatch – 'Lydia's had an idea, haven't you, Lydia?'

'Yes,' said Lydia, walking over to where Roo was sitting. 'I'm sure this little girl could manage a short line of dialogue, couldn't you, dear?'

'*Me?*' asked Roo, in a squeak.

'Yes, all you have to say is, "Poor thing. I wish I could do something to help." You can manage that, can't you?'

'No,' said Roo faintly.

'Splendid. I'll send someone to take you over to costume and make-up.' The woman walked off again.

'You're squeezing me,' said Attlee.

'Sorry,' said Roo, releasing her grip. 'But I can't.'

'Can't what?'

'Act. I just can't.'

'I'm rather afraid you'll have to. We're inside a wish, and I assume we have to go along with the narrative. Was the space rocket story in the book called "Veronica Saves the Ship" or was it called "Veronica Plunges to her Doom after Failing to Work Out a Sum and Bursting into Tears"? Was the story we're in now called "Unexpected Film Star" or was it called "Film Studio Closes with the Loss of a Hundred Jobs when Girl Refuses to Attempt a Single Line"?'

'But you don't understand – I'm no good at acting. I only ever played a tree at school. Ed or Willard should be doing this, not me.'

'It's ten words,' said Attlee. *Poor thing. I wish I could do something to help.* Try it. Remember to add a little note of sympathy and sadness.'

'Poor thing,' repeated Roo. 'I wish I could do something to help.'

There was a pause.

'Are you still playing a tree?' asked Attlee.

'Hello there!' said a young woman, tapping towards them on high heels. 'I'm Vivian and I'm here to take you to hair and make-up. You can leave your kitty-cat here,' she said, just as Attlee's stomach gave an incredibly loud gurgle. Roo lifted him off her lap, but he wriggled at the last minute and fell the last few inches to the floor.

'Are you all right?' asked Roo.

'Smelly, isn't he?' said Vivian. Attlee gave them both a look and walked away, limping slightly, and Roo followed the woman to a corner of the studio, where there was a table and a mirror surrounded by light bulbs.

'Sit down,' said Vivian, picking up a hairbrush. 'You must be ever so excited.'

Roo attempted the word 'yes' and it came out as 'ung'.

She stared at herself in the mirror; she looked terrified, her face pinched with nerves.

'I think I'll put a little bow in your hair,' said Vivian, peering at a box of ribbons and hairgrips, and picking out a length of scarlet silk. 'Do you like this one?'

'Ung,' said Roo again, but something in the box had caught her eye. Lying between a purple hairnet and a yellow clip in the shape of a daffodil was a familiar tortoiseshell hairslide. It was exactly like the one Miss Filey wore every day.

Wonderingly, Roo picked it up. A grey hair was caught in the hinge.

'I found that on the set this morning,' said Vivian. 'Do you know who it belongs to?'

'Yes,' said Roo. She closed her hand over the slide, as if it was a good-luck charm.

Five minutes later, with her face plastered with powder and her hair in a bow, Roo stood in front of a piece of wood painted to look like railings. She was wearing a thick winter coat, even though the studio lights made it feel like a summer's day, and she was standing next to a woman who was supposed to be her mother.

'GOING FOR A REHEARSAL,' shouted someone.

The director knelt down beside her. 'Now, I want you to fix your eyes just to the right of the camera, and pretend you're watching poor little Emmeline being thrown out of her house. And when I shout "Action!", count to three in your head, and then say your line. OK?'

'Ung,' said Roo, fixing her gaze just to the right of

the camera, where there was an empty chair on which someone had left a plate containing half a sandwich. Her heart was beating so fast it felt as if an alarm clock was going off in her chest.

'Let's go, then. *Action!*'

Roo counted to three and opened her mouth, hoping the right words would come out. What came out was an incredibly loud burp. 'Sorry,' she said, mortified, clamping a hand over her lips.

'Not to worry,' said the director. 'It's just a rehearsal. Take your eyeline again.'

'That means, look in the right direction,' muttered the actress playing her mother.

Roo looked at the chair and rehearsed the line in her head. *Poor thing. I wish I could do something to help. Poor thing. I wish I could do something to help.* If she could just get the first couple of words right, then the rest would follow.

'And ACTION!'

Poor thing. Poor thing. Poor thing. NOW!

'Thore ping,' she said quite clearly. Someone sighed. 'Sorry,' said Roo again.

'Have another go,' said the director encouragingly, but Roo could see him checking his watch as he spoke. She took a long, deep breath.

'And ACTION!'

'PoorthingIwishIcoulddosomethingtohelp,' said Roo immediately, all the words bursting out in a single noise. 'Sorry,' she added. 'That was too fast, wasn't it?'

The director nodded and managed an unconvincing smile, and then he turned away towards the cameraman. Roo, embarrassed, looked down at the very shiny lace-up shoes she'd been given to wear, and overheard the whispered exchange between the two men.

I'm afraid this was probably a mistake. We'll have to lose the scene.

'What about if I turn on the camera without the kid knowing? You can pretend you're still rehearsing, and if she keeps on saying it, we might get something we can use.'

'Good idea.' The director turned back. 'Let's have another go,' he said quite kindly, but Roo could sense desperation in the air. She saw the man with the microphone glance at the make-up woman and shake his head gloomily. Beginning to panic, Roo gripped Miss Filey's hairclip so hard that she could feel the metal prongs digging into her palm.

'Take your eyeline, please,' said the director, and Roo looked at the empty chair, and saw that Attlee was walking very slowly towards it, clearly in some pain, one of his back legs dragging. As he neared the chair, he lifted his nose, scenting the sandwich that was sitting on a plate on the seat. Then, realizing that he couldn't reach it, he turned away, head drooping.

'And ACTION!' said the director.

Roo couldn't take her eyes off Attlee. He limped a step further and then sank slowly, despairingly, to the floor, his chest heaving with laboured breath, his eyes half-closed.

'Poor thing,' said Roo, her voice trembling a little. 'Oh, I wish I could do something to help.' She felt a feathery tickle on her cheek and raised a hand to brush it away. It was a tear.

'And CUT!' shouted the director. 'Did we get that?'

'Got it,' said the cameraman.

'Incredible. *Incredible!*'

Roo looked around in amazement. People were clapping.

'You're a natural,' said the woman with the clipboard.

'I almost cried myself,' said the woman with the tea trolley. 'You were fifty times better than that horrid little spoiled brat who's playing the star role.'

'Can I just check on my cat?' asked Roo, hurrying past the camera and kneeling down beside Attlee. 'Are you badly hurt?' she whispered, bending down beside him.

He opened one eye. 'Did they get the shot?'

'What?'

'Did they film your line?'

'Yes,' said Roo, turning to look at the film crew. They were still clapping. 'They all thought I was really good.'

'Excellent,' said Attlee, getting up and stretching. 'Could you hand me that sandwich?'

'I thought you were hurt!'

'Acting,' said Attlee.

'Someone call Davina's agent,' the director was saying. 'We need to cancel her contract and get this little girl to star instead. There's a big, big future ahead of her!'

Roo found herself grinning hugely. She reached for the sandwich, but as she grabbed it, the plate and the chair seemed to dissolve into the air, the camera and the sound booms folded and dwindled, and she was sitting on the bed in Miss Filey's room, with a sandwich in her hand and Attlee standing on the rug in front of her.

She held out the sandwich to him.

'Oh, it's cheese spread,' said Attlee disappointedly. 'I shan't bother.'

CHAPTER 21

E d and Willard looked towards the three big rocks, two triangular and one bun-shaped, which poked out of the sea at the rear of the island, just beside a sheer cliff. 'Can you read out that bit from the book again?' asked Ed. 'About the cave.'

Willard found the right page.

Delia looked back at the narrow mouth of the cave. If it hadn't been for the adventurous seal and the clever clues, she'd never have got past the rocks and found the entrance.

'OK. So which seal is it?' asked Ed.

Almost the entire surface of each rock was covered with seals, all basking in the sunlight. More seals bobbed in the sea beside them. Yet more were clustered around the boat, upright in the water, their doggy faces staring unblinkingly at the boys.

'How can we tell if a seal's adventurous?' asked Ed broodingly. 'They're hardly going to be posting photos of themselves bungee-jumping, are they?'

They'd sailed right round the island, looking for a place to land, and had then turned back to where the rocks loomed out of the water – these, presumably, were the three shapes on the map, guarding the entrance to a cave. Waves slapped regularly between them, but the gaps were far too narrow for the boat to pass through.

'We need to think,' said Ed. He pointed the boat into the light wind, and loosened the rope so that the sail flapped freely and they bobbed gently on the spot. 'Let's have a look at the map again.' He studied the drawing and realized that there was something slightly odd about it. The island and the rocks were simply inked outlines, nothing fancy about them, but the sea was filled with lots of carefully drawn fish, each perched on its own little wave. 'Look,' he said, showing it to Willard. 'Why would someone spend more time drawing the fish in the sea than the island?'

'Maybe they're just really good at fishes,' said Willard. 'It's like my mum taught me how to draw a flamingo, so I put flamingoes in everything.'

'And why are all the fish in bunches of three?' continued Ed, ignoring this. 'Nine bunches of three.'

A series of splashes made them look up. All the seals on the bun-shaped rock were sliding off it, into the water – all except one, who lay right on top of it, head raised, its expression full of anticipation.

'It's waiting for something,' said Willard. 'Look at its face – it's the way people look at the top of a roller coaster.'

A gentle wave splashed against the base of the rock. A few seconds later came another gentle wave. A few seconds after that a huge curl of water rose with a roar and completely submerged the whole rock, lifting the seal like a leaf on its surface.

'It's *surfing!*' shouted Willard. The seal, its expression ecstatic, was whirled away and seemed to disappear momentarily. And then the water settled, and it swam into view again.

'Now *that's* an adventurous seal,' said Ed.

'Can we do that?' asked Willard.

'Do what?'

'Surf over it. In the boat, I mean. Get to the other side of the rocks that way.'

Ed went quiet, his eyes fixed on the bun-shaped rock. The seals were climbing back on.

'Or is that a stupid idea?' asked Willard. 'I never really know.'

'No. It's a good one, a brilliant one. THREE.'

'Three what?'

'I'm counting waves. Something's occurred to me. Watch how they hit the rock. There's a small wave . . . and then another small wave . . . and then a bigger one.'

'But not big enough to surf over.'

'No – but maybe that really, really big wave occurs regularly. The seals knew it was coming. And the map! The fish on the map are in groups of three, aren't they?'

'Yup.' Willard pored over it. 'Nine groups of three.'

'So maybe every twenty-seventh wave is the one. Let's go for it. I think we're up to number fourteen now,' Ed added, still counting, 'and now a bigger one . . . fifteen.'

He tightened the sail and steered the boat nearer to the rock.

'See this thing,' he said to Willard, pointing to a ridge on the floor between them. 'It's the top of a long, thin slab of wood that sticks out underneath the boat and stops us drifting. It's called the centreboard. When the seals jump off the rock, you'll have to lift it up really quickly.'

'Why?'

'Because if you don't, it'll catch on the rock, rip off the entire bottom of the boat and we'll sink instantly.'

'Right,' said Willard. 'That's quite a big responsibility, isn't it? I mean, compared to the things I'm normally told to do. Like "tidy your bedroom" or "rinse plates before you put them in the dishwasher".'

'Or "don't leave your school bag in the middle of the floor",' suggested Ed. 'I get that a lot.'

Willard nodded. 'Or "make sure you put your football kit in the washing machine".'

There was a pause. Ed raised one eyebrow.

'You probably don't get told that,' said Willard.

A series of rapid splashes made them both look round. The seals (all except one) were sliding off the rock.

'Get ready,' shouted Ed, moving the tiller so that the boat was pointed directly at the rock. 'It must be the next wave or the one after. Pull up the centreboard!'

Willard gripped and hauled, and in one smooth movement raised the plate of wood, just as the steady, gentle splash of the waves changed to a slow roar. 'I did it!' he shouted. The boat began to lift. 'Here we go!'

The water, green and glassy, rose over the rock, taking the boat with it and launching it down the other side. Spray burst over the boat, blinding them.

'Hang on tight!' shouted Ed. The cliff face was suddenly directly ahead

Willard gripped his seat, as the boat veered sideways, caught in an invisible current. It spun in a complete circle, bounced a few times and then settled – and they were bobbing gently in a calm patch of water, between a curtain of rock and the mouth of the hidden cave.

And in the middle of the boat, between Ed and Willard, was a large seal.

CHAPTER 22

Willard stared at the seal. It had reared up on its front flippers, and was looking around the boat with interest, and it was so large that Willard couldn't see over it to where Ed was sitting.

'Are you there, Ed?' he called.

'Yes.'

'Did you know seals were this big?'

'No.' Ed looked up at the enormous slab of animal right next to him, its skin like a soaked carpet. He could feel the cold saltiness of the air around it. 'I think it might be a species called an elephant seal.'

'What do they eat?' asked Willard slightly nervously.

'Fish, mainly, I think. But we probably shouldn't do anything to annoy it.'

'But it might get annoyed at something really random. I mean, I had a teacher in my last school who went mad if I did a creaky door impression whenever she opened a cupboard. And there was another one who—'

'Have you got the book?' interrupted Ed. 'It might say in there.'

'The book?' Willard looked around. 'Oh. The seal's sitting on it.' He could just see the crumpled page they'd been reading, sticking out from under one flipper. 'But the paddle's here and we know we have to go into the cave, don't we?' He groped around under his seat and pulled it out and was about to dip it into the water, when he noticed something. 'There are funny marks on this paddle,' he said.

'What sort of marks?'

Willard tilted the handle to catch the sunlight. 'Scratches,' he said. 'Nine lots of three scratches in a row.'

'Nine threes are twenty-seven! Someone else was counting the waves!'

'And there are letters too. R . . . F.'

'Miss Filey again – she was here too! She's done this wish as well!'

'On her own again,' said Willard. 'I wouldn't want to do that.'

'Nor me,' said Ed. He heard the soft dip of Willard's paddle stroking the water, and he took the tiller and began to steer. The boat nosed into the cleft in the cliff-face; ahead was a broad flooded cave, lit by a slender shaft of sunlight from a hole in the roof. Beyond the sunlight, the cave narrowed into darkness. The seal shifted slightly, and Ed watched hopefully to see if it was going to slither off into the water, but instead it lay down with a long sigh and closed its eyes.

'Make yourself at home,' muttered Ed. He and Willard could see each other now over the smooth, furry bulk.

'There's supposed to be treasure at the end of this,' said Willard.

The cave was narrower now, so it felt as if they were travelling along a sunken river – and they seemed to be moving quite quickly, though Willard wasn't paddling particularly fast. Ed reached out a hand and touched the wall; the rock was deathly cold and sticky with salt. Ahead, another thin sunbeam pierced the darkness, and he looked up as they passed through it and saw a fissure in the rock, and – far, far above – a tiny shred of blue sky. The passage bent to the left and narrowed yet again, so that the boat bumped against the walls and Willard could barely insert his paddle into the gap. 'But we're still moving,' he said. 'Why are we going so fast?'

'I think the tide must be coming in,' said Ed, just as the boat nosed into a small round chamber. The ceiling was quite low – only a few inches higher than the mast – and it was pierced with cracks, so that a lattice of light lit the water. The boat stopped moving forward and began to rock and spin.

'What's that?' exclaimed Willard, pointing to an object sticking out of the water at the centre of the chamber; something metallic on top of it was catching the light. Willard paddled towards it.

'A chest!' he said. 'A treasure chest!' Now that they were closer, they could see that the base of it was bolted to a rock. The wood was darkly stained and on the top was a four-pointed star, marked with gold letters: N, E, S, W.

'Compass points,' said Ed.

Willard leaned out over the edge of the boat and tried to lift the lid.

'It's locked.' He fiddled with the letters. 'They move when you press them. They click down.'

'You must have to do them in a certain order,' said Ed. 'I bet it says in the book. Can you see it at all?'

Willard peered at what he could see of the page beneath the seal's flipper. 'OK,' he said.

'I must have to press the compass points in order,' said Delia. 'But which order? There must be a clue.' On impulse, she held up the map to the light, and gasped. A faint line of letters was visible. First an 'S', then a—

'Then a what?' asked Ed urgently.

'I can't see. It's all flipper after that,' said Willard. 'But we've got that map, haven't we?' He looked around for it. Ed looked around for it. Their eyes met over the top of the seal.

'I think it must have got washed away when we went over the rocks,' said Ed quietly.

There was a sudden thump from above, and the boat jolted violently.

'The mast!' shouted Ed, craning his head back. 'The mast's banging against the ceiling. The water's still rising!'

There was a second scraping thump and this time the boat tilted slightly.

Ed looked at Willard over the top of the seal. 'We have to finish the story and get out of here fast, because this is properly dangerous.'

Willard's eyes widened, and then he knelt forward in the boat and tapped the seal on its shoulder. 'You've got to move,' he said. 'Go on, get off.'

It stared back at him. Its eyes reminded Willard of black fruit gums. 'Have you got any sweets in your pockets?' he asked Ed and began to rummage through in his own. 'Maybe we can bribe him, maybe we . . .' His fingers closed over an unexpected object and he drew it out as triumphantly as if it had been a priceless diamond. 'Look!' he said, holding it up, awe-struck. 'A Fishee Treat! I forgot I picked it up – it's the one that fell off the table!' He reached forward and waved it near the seal's nose until its whiskers began to twitch. 'Go on, then,' he said, flicking the treat into the water. 'Fetch!'

In one fluid movement, the seal poured itself over the edge and into the water. Without its weight, the boat seemed to spring upwards and there was a loud, splintering crack as the top of the mast broke off.

Ed grabbed the book and the soaked page tore in half. He held the pieces together. 'S-N-N-E-W-W-S,' he said.

Willard leaned over as far as he dared. 'S-N-N . . .' he said, pressing the letters on the chest. 'Then what?' The boat was beginning to tip; the remains of the mast were wedged against the rock ceiling and water started to slop around their feet.

'E-W-W-S,' shouted Ed. 'Hurry up!!'

'E . . . W . . . W . . .' The boat lurched and began to fill. Willard lost his balance and caught hold of the chest with one hand. One foot was still in the boat but the other was pedalling in the water, with nothing beneath it but swirling darkness.

'S!' shouted Ed, grabbing the mast with one hand, and with the other, lifting the book above his head. '*S!*'

And Willard lunged forward and pressed the final letter.

There was a loud snap and the chest sprang open. In it were jewelled chains and ropes of pearls and a ruby brooch the size of his clenched fist and a gold shell lined with the rainbow glint of mother-of-pearl and suddenly he was standing ankle-deep in the pond in Miss Filey's garden, wet from the chest down and blinking at the brightness of the daylight, with Ed parked right next to him, the wheelchair up to its footplates in water.

'We did it!' he shouted, his voice cracking with excitement.

'We did it,' said Ed, astonished. His whole body was trembling with the tension of the last few minutes.

He unclasped his right hand from a mast that was no longer there and then held it up towards Willard. 'High five.'

Willard started to lift his own right hand, but there was something in it – something small but surprisingly weighty.

'Hang on,' he began to say, but Ed was already trying to manoeuvre himself out of the pond. Without success.

'I'm stuck in the mud, you'll have to help me,' he said stiffly; he always hated having to ask people.

Willard uncurled his fingers, glimpsed the glint of the gold shell, and then stuffed into his pocket. 'OK,' he said. 'Do you want me to pull or push?'

CHAPTER 23

Roo opened the door of the bedroom and peered into the hall.

'Ed?' she called. 'Willard?' She could see a note on the floor, and she took a cautious step towards it, just as the front door smacked open and Willard burst in, with Ed just behind him.

'You're back!' said Ed, hugely relieved. 'Where did you go?'

'Why are you wet?' asked Roo.

'What's all that powder stuff on your face?' asked Willard.

'Where's Attlee?' asked Attlee, strolling into the hall. 'I thought I'd ask, since it's clear nobody else is going to. "Is Attlee hungry?" Yet another unasked question.'

'I found a Fishee Treat,' said Willard, 'but I gave it to a huge seal.'

'Highly believable,' said Attlee. 'I think there may be some of the more inferior cat food still in the kitchen.'

'But if we go in there, it might turn into a rocket again.'

'Did it happen immediately last time?' asked Attlee. 'Did we shoot skywards in the three seconds it would take you to reach the bottom shelf of the cupboard beside the window?'

'It's a risk, though,' said Ed.

'I'll go,' said Roo. 'I wouldn't be back here now if it wasn't for Attlee.'

'No, don't,' called Ed, but she'd already gone, racing through the kitchen door and straight across to the cupboard, jerking the box of food from the shelf and running back again.

'It was fine,' she said, kneeling down by Attlee and shaking some treats onto the floor beside him.

Willard told her about the sailing boat, and the seal, and then she explained about the film studio and the moment when everyone applauded her performance, even though she hadn't really been acting at all, and it seemed to Ed that since he'd last seen his sister she'd grown somehow older, or taller. Or maybe she was just more confident.

'I've never had an adventure on my own before,' she said.

'You still haven't,' said Attlee pointedly, his mouth full of Happee Kittee Prawn-Flavoured Bics.

'Sorry, I meant an adventure without another human there. This thing's really hot,' she added, unbuttoning the winter coat she'd been given at the studio. 'Do you think it's stealing, accidentally taking something from a wish?'

'No, definitely not,' said Willard, checking his pocket to make sure the gold shell was still there.

'We need to keep moving,' said Ed. 'We didn't find Miss Filey, but we found evidence that she'd been in the boat before us. *And* we realized that the sum in the rocket was in her handwriting, so she'd been in that adventure too.'

'*And* she'd been in the studio!' said Roo. 'I found her hairclip.'

'So, we just need to catch up with her. We have to hurry up and jump into another wish.'

'But shouldn't you get dry first?' said Roo. 'Or at least sit on a towel.'

'All right, Mum,' said Ed sarcastically, but he moved towards the bathroom anyway. 'We should all go in together,' he said. 'Just in case it suddenly turns into a castle or something.'

They found a pile of towels in the bathroom cupboard and Willard and Ed attempted to blot themselves dry.

'We could put your jeans in the tumble dryer,' said Roo.

'There is no tumble dryer in this house,' called Attlee, from the hall.

'And anyway,' said Ed, 'I'm not risking turning up in an avalanche with no trousers on.'

Willard started laughing.

'Or a zoo,' added Ed. 'Hey, Willard – what does a tiger do if he sees you in your underwear?'

'Dunno,' said Willard.

'Pants,' said Ed, and Willard laughed so hard that he fell on the floor.

Roo, washing the caked layer of make-up from her face, glimpsed Ed in the mirror. He was grinning. It normally took him ages to get comfortable with new people, but he and Willard seemed suddenly like old mates.

'Right, so where should we go next?' asked Ed. 'It's clear nothing's going to happen in here.'

'Maybe Miss Filey only imagined wishes happening in important rooms,' said Willard, who'd never rated baths.

'How about the living room?' suggested Roo.

Ed nodded. 'Good idea.'

They found Attlee curled up on the sofa, sound asleep, his usual smell of fishiness overlaid with a new layer of prawniness.

'So now we just wait, do we?' asked Willard. 'Weird to think that it all started in this room, with the dog. And then the ant. And then flying, except that we didn't, really. And then . . .' He tried to remember.

'The scratch on the table,' said Roo. 'We tried to give Miss Filey a really small wish, so it wouldn't shock her. But it accidentally turned into Attlee talking.'

'All our wishes were small,' said Ed. 'And all of Miss Filey's were huge and complicated and adventurous. She's better at wishing than we are.' He checked the pocket of his wheelchair to make sure the book was back in there, and then looked up as the door to the hall suddenly slammed shut. 'We're on,' he said, feeling breathless. 'Here comes another wish.'

Roo clutched Ed's shoulder. Willard braced himself. Attlee gave a slight snore.

'Note the delicate, lacy appearance of the rose

petals,' said someone behind them, and the children spun round to see a woman pointing at the picture of a vase of flowers that hung on the wall of Miss Filey's living room. Except that the wall was shooting out sideways in both directions, and the ceiling was rising, and they were somewhere else altogether . . .

CHAPTER 24

'An *art gallery*?' whispered Willard, looking around.
'I wouldn't exactly call that an *adventure*.'

The three of them were standing in a small crowd,
being lectured by a smiling elderly woman in a flowery
frock, a handbag over her arm. 'So how do we think
this painting technique was achieved?' she asked,
looking enquiringly at her audience.

No one answered. She moved her gaze along the
crowd and, to Willard's horror, fixed her eyes on him.

'What would you say, young man? Do you think
that this particular artist used a . . . *brush*?' She said the
last word with great emphasis and raised her eyebrows
as she did so. Willard recognized her expression; it was

the same one that teachers used when they were asking a trick question, like: 'So is a hundred and thirty-one an . . . *even* number???'

'No,' said Willard confidently.

'That's absolutely right. So, what do you think the artist used *instead* of a brush? It was something *quite* unlikely. Have a guess.'

'A banana?' suggested Willard. Ed, who had started looking through the adventure stories book, let out a great snort of laughter, and the lecturer turned away slightly, so that she was addressing the other half of the crowd.

'It was a feather,' she said rather frostily. 'Now, let's move on to a very important painting in the next room. Follow me.' The little crowd trotted after her. 'Is there a funny smell in here?' said one of them to a companion. 'Sort of fishy?'

Roo looked around hurriedly and was relieved to see Attlee curled up on one end of a padded seat in the centre of the gallery.

'*I've already found the story,*' whispered Ed, beckoning the other two towards him, 'and it's about a robbery. It's called "Belinda Solves a Crime".' He swivelled the book round to show them a picture. A girl was peering around the edge of a large metal sculpture, watching two men in hats. One of the men was short and slight, and one was huge and square-shouldered; the short one was furtively removing a painting of a horse from the wall.

Ed turned the book back towards himself and flicked through the pages; the paper was still stained and dimpled from the sea water. 'Yes, this girl Belinda spots these really suspicious-looking men stealing a famous painting – the big man hides the picture on his back, under his coat, with the string round his neck. So then she follows them towards the exit, tricks them somehow into going into a cleaning cupboard, locks the door and phones the police. She ends up getting a medal or something.' He showed them another illustration of Belinda, in which she was shaking hands with an important-looking mayor.

'Let's go, then!' said Willard. 'It should be dead easy to spot those two.'

'But we need to check if Miss Filey's here,' said Roo. 'I'll look all around for her, shall I, and then find you?' And she was off before Ed had even finished nodding, excited to be speeding away on her own again. She headed in the same direction that the lecturer had taken. The crowd had gathered around a painting in the next room, and as Roo hurried past, she caught a glimpse of a small picture of a glass bowl containing two goldfish. 'Despite its size,' the lecturer was saying, 'this is one of the most valuable paintings in the gallery. Some might say it was the jewel of our collection . . .'

Ed and Willard went in the opposite direction to Roo. The next room contained only a uniformed guard, dozing on a chair, and there were no people at all in the one after that, though it felt quite full thanks to a very large metal sculpture, pierced with holes and placed right at the centre.

'Hey, look,' said Willard, pointing at the far wall. 'Isn't that the horse painting the men were stealing in the book?'

'That's the one,' said Ed. 'Brilliant! I wonder if . . . stay there a moment.' Cautiously he edged towards the door to the next room, until he could see through the glass panel. *'It's them!'* he hissed. *'Don't let them spot you.'*

Willard crouched, and looked over Ed's shoulder. The two men, one very large, in a coat, one small, with a moustache, were standing talking in front of a painting. Coat Man was holding a gallery guidebook, while Moustache seemed to be sketching on a pad of paper. A minute or so went by. The two men moved very slowly from picture to picture. Ed used the time to flick through the storybook again.

'What I don't understand is, how are we supposed to trap them in a cupboard?' whispered Willard, who'd been eyeing up the enormous size of Coat Man.

'I've just checked that bit,' said Ed. 'They ask Belinda the way out, and she points them towards the broom cupboard instead of the exit and when they go in, she turns the key.'

'But that big one could just lean on a door with one finger and it would, like, break in half. And anyway, wouldn't they notice all the brooms?'

'I know,' said Ed uneasily. He thought for a moment. 'I've got an idea,' he said. 'Why don't you go and phone the police right now and tell them a robbery's in progress. That way, maybe the thieves'll get caught on the way out and we won't have to do the cupboard thing.'

'I don't have a phone,' said Willard.

'Nobody's got a phone,' said Ed. 'All Miss Filey's stories are set in the olden days. There's no CCTV here and no one's got a computer, or a tablet or a phone.'

'So how do I call the police?'

'Use a public phone box.'

Willard had never in his life used a public phone box. 'I haven't got any money,' he said.

'It's nine-nine-nine, you don't need money.'

'OK. But why can't *you* do it?'

Ed took a deep breath. 'Because in a phone box, the phone is quite high up, so I'd have to pull myself to standing and people would notice and start trying to help me, and instead of making a secret phone call it would be like a great big audience show called "Ed makes a phone call". All right?'

'All right,' said Willard. 'I get it. Sorry.'

'It's OK.'

'So, what are you going to do while I'm doing that?'

'I'm going to wait till they steal the painting and then I'll knock the big one over by ramming him with my wheelchair before tying his hands together with one of my shoelaces and then – just kidding,' he added, and Willard grinned. 'No, I'm just going to keep an eye on them.'

Willard sprinted off in search of a phone box and Ed watched the men for a moment longer before moving back from the door and hiding himself behind the sculpture. Another couple of minutes went by and then he heard the door open. He tilted his head so that he could see through one of the holes. The two thieves came into the room and went straight over to the horse painting.

'That's the one,' said Moustache.

'Oh, yes,' said Coat. 'Yes, that's tremendous.'

'Look at the shine on that stallion.'

'And look at his face. That's a noble horse, that is.'

'And lively. You can practically hear him neighing.'

'Who's it by?'

'Stubbs.'

'Stubbs?'

'Yes, George Stubbs. Worth a bit, I'd say.'

There was a pause while they looked at it again.

'Lovely,' said Coat. 'Really lovely. So, shall I show you *my* favourite picture now?'

'Go on then. And then we'd better get going if we want to see that film.'

And, leaving the horse painting untouched on the wall, they walked out of the room. Ed stared at the closing door in disbelief, and then hurried out from behind the sculpture and went over to the painting, just to double-check that it hadn't been stolen. It hadn't. He looked at the illustration in the book again and felt a surge of worry. Something had gone very badly wrong.

CHAPTER 25

There was a red phone box directly outside the gallery, in a small courtyard separated from the street by railings. Willard opened the heavy door and stepped into the little booth. The first thing he saw was a large metal box fixed to the back wall, with two buttons on it, labelled 'A' and 'B'. On a shelf at shoulder height, next to it, was a large black, shiny object that was presumably the telephone.

It was in two parts which were connected by a sort of plaited rope; the top part was shaped a bit like one of the mini dumbbells his mother used in weights classes. He picked it up and it buzzed loudly. The bottom part was vaguely triangular and had a metal circle fixed to

the front of it, pierced with small holes. A number was visible at the bottom of each hole. He pressed '9' but nothing happened.

There was a notice just above the telephone, which read 'TO SPEAK TO OPERATOR, PUSH BUTTON A', and he pushed it.

'Hellay, ken Ay hilp yew?' said a woman's voice, in an impossibly posh accent.

'I need to phone the police.'

'Yew'll hev to dayle nane-nane-nane.'

'What?'

'Yew'll hev to dayle *nane-nane-nane*.'

'Oh, you mean "nine-nine-nine"? I know, but I can't work the phone. Can you call them for me?'

'Ay'm sorry, but ez Ay say, yew'll hev to dayle nane-nane-nane.'

Willard jabbed at the number again. 'But it doesn't work!' he said, his voice rising in frustration.

There was a knock on the door.

'Need help, sonny?' asked a friendly voice. 'I was just passing and you sound all upset.'

'Yes,' said Willard, opening the door, 'I have to phone the police, and—' He stopped speaking and stared. It was the big man with the coat from the gallery. Just behind him was the small man with the moustache.

'The police?' said Coat Man. 'That sounds important. Want me to do it for you?' Willard felt as if he'd been turned to stone – or something less solid than stone, something that might crumble if accidentally leaned on: a digestive biscuit, possibly. Coat Man eased the phone from Willard's hand and reached round him, pushing a finger into the '9' hole and dragging it round, so that the whole metal circle revolved.

'Oh, you *turn* it,' said Willard, watching, paralysed, as Coat Man did it twice more.

'Hello?' said Coat Man, into the phone. 'Police please. A lad here needs to speak to them.' He handed the dumbbell shape to Willard. 'Tell them why you need the police,' he said encouragingly.

Willard's mouth felt as dry as when he'd once eaten three cream crackers for a challenge. 'Hello,' he said croakily. 'There's been a' – he turned away from Coat Man – '*a robbery,*' he whispered, *'at the art gallery.'*

'Can you speak up?' said a voice from the phone. 'You're very quiet.'

'*Someone's stolen a painting from the art gallery,*' said Willard, slightly more loudly.

'Someone's stolen a painting from the gallery?' shouted Coat Man, horrified.

'What?' said Moustache, sticking his head round the door of the phone booth. 'What's happened?'

'This lad saw someone steal a painting.'

'Which painting?' asked the person on the other end of the phone.

'*I think it was a horse,*' croaked Willard.

'Not the *horse!*' shouted Moustache, horrified.

'And when did this happen?' asked the person on the other end of the phone.

'Er . . . just now,' said Willard hesitantly.

'Just *now*?' repeated Coat Man. 'Excuse me, lad,' he said, taking the phone from Willard's hand again and raising it to his own mouth. 'Save the questions till later, you need to get here right away,' he said loudly and sternly. 'This is an emergency!' He slammed the phone down and nodded with satisfaction. 'Right, the police are on their way. Now, lad – tell us everything that happened.'

Roo had searched everywhere, including the gift shop and the ladies' loos, but had failed to find Miss Filey. As she jogged back towards her starting point, she passed the tour group, all clustered round a sculpture of a woman with three heads. 'So, before we finish, does anyone have any final questions?' the lecturer was asking.

Attlee had woken up and was sitting on the back of the padded bench, looking fixedly at something and dribbling slightly. He glanced at Roo as she approached and then switched his gaze back to the same point as before, and she saw that he was staring through an archway at the small painting of two goldfish on the wall of the next room. The lecturer came into view again, on her own this time, her handbag still over her arm. She stopped to look at the picture of the fish.

'I have two questions,' said Attlee as Roo turned back to him. 'The first question is, "How long must we stay here?" and the second is, "Where are the other two and what are they doing?" If the answer to the first question is "only a minute or two longer", then you don't need to bother with the other one.'

'But the answer to the first question depends on the answer to the second question,' said Roo.

'Oh, very clever,' said Attlee waspishly, twitching his tail while continuing to look over her shoulder at the painted goldfish. 'Very smart. And of no help whatsoever.'

'*Ed* always wakes up cross,' said Roo.

'Does he? Why has that fact any relevance to me?'

'Because you've just woken up and you're cross.'

There was a pause, during which Attlee continued to look over her shoulder.

'So, would you like me to answer the second question?' asked Roo.

'If it's not too much trouble.'

She ignored the sarcastic tone. 'The wish we're in is about a painting being stolen from this gallery, so Ed and Willard are looking out for the thieves.'

'Thieves? In the plural?'

'Yes. Two men.'

'Not one older lady, in a frock?'

'No.'

'Are you sure? Because, over the last thirty seconds I've just seen someone of that description take a small penknife out of her handbag, remove a picture from its frame, roll it up and walk away.'

'*What???*' Roo spun round. On the wall in the next room, instead of a painting of two goldfish, there was now an empty wooden rectangle . . .

CHAPTER 26

'But that's not the story in the book!' said Roo, squeaky with shock. 'It's supposed to be a picture of a horse and it's supposed to be stolen by two men.' She ran towards the empty picture frame, looked around wildly, and saw, trotting away through the next room, the lecturer in the flowery dress.

'I'll be back,' she hissed to Attlee, and hurried after the woman, trying to keep her own footsteps light and noiseless. The lecturer seemed to be following the signs towards the exit, and Roo trailed her at a distance. They passed through two more rooms and then entered a huge, long hall, hung with paintings.

'Hey! Roo!'

Roo turned to see Ed coming through an archway on the other side. She put a finger to her lips. The lecturer was heading for the revolving door marked 'EXIT', but when she was just metres from reaching it, the door started to move, and into the room came Willard. He was looking distinctly bewildered. Immediately after him came a very large man in a coat, and then a very small man with a moustache, and then a policeman, and then another policeman and then a third policeman.

Gallery visitors stopped and stared, but the lecturer smoothly turned on her heel and went quietly over to one side of the huge hall, where a litter bin stood against the wall. With no one but Roo watching her, she opened her handbag and fumbled through it, taking out an object like a folded pillowcase. Without looking, she dropped it into the bin, and then followed it with another object, smaller and heavier than the first. Then she snapped her handbag shut and walked briskly over to the policemen, who were talking to Willard.

'Hello,' she said loudly and clearly. 'How may I help you? I'm Mabel Collins, one of the senior curators of this gallery.'

'This boy says there's been a robbery,' said the most

senior of the policemen, who was wearing a uniform glittering with silver braids.

'Yup, that's what he told us,' said Coat Man, nodding vigorously. 'He said someone had stolen a painting.'

'Of a horse,' added Moustache.

'*No*,' said Ed, scooting rapidly towards them. 'No, he's made a mistake. No one's stolen a painting.' He caught Willard's eye, and shook his head frantically.

'Haven't they?' asked Willard, totally confused.

'No, they haven't,' said Ed.

'Yes, they have!' said a squeaky voice.

Everyone turned to look at the speaker. It was Roo, standing up very straight, her expression stiff with nerves. In one hand she was holding what looked like a folded pillowcase, and in the other, a penknife. 'Look!' she said, giving the folded object a shake. It unrolled, and everyone gasped.

'What have you done?' wailed Mabel Collins, clasping her hands. 'The Matisse goldfish! You have *ripped* a great work of genius from its frame.'

'It wasn't me,' said Roo. 'It was you! You put it in your bag, and then when you saw the police, you dropped it in this bin. I expect you were going to collect it later, when the police had left.'

'As if anyone would believe that. I have devoted my

life to art.' Mabel walked up to Roo and gently removed the canvas from her hand. 'If this is damaged,' she said, her voice trembling, 'you will be liable to the cost of restoration, and you will be paying for it for the *rest of your life*. And now I'm sure the police have a few questions for you.'

'Hang on,' said Ed loudly, hurrying to Roo's side. 'If my sister said she saw you steal this, then it means you stole it. She doesn't tell lies.'

'Did *you* see the theft take place?' asked the policeman.

'No,' said Ed, rather defiantly.

'Did anyone else see it?'

'Yes,' said Roo. 'Attlee did.'

'And who's Attlee?'

There was a long pause. Roo blushed. 'He's a cat,' she said, in a very small voice.

Mabel Collins gave a dismissive snort. 'If you don't mind, officer, I shall take this painting immediately to the restoration wing.'

'We'll need a statement from you first, madam,' said the senior policeman, taking out his notebook. 'And then we need a good long chat with the young lady.'

'*That woman really did steal it*,' whispered Roo to Ed.

'*I know, I believe you.*'

'*So what do we do?*'

'*I don't know – this is nothing like the story in the book. It's like someone's rewritten it.*'

Willard had sidled up to them. '*What's happening?*' he asked, out of the corner of his mouth.

'*We don't know.*'

'*Why isn't it like the book?*'

'*We don't know.*'

'*Am I going to prison?*' asked Roo.

'No!' said both Willard and Ed, loudly and fiercely, and as they spoke there was a sudden flurry of movement over by the door. Two men in smart suits came in and positioned themselves on either side. They looked, thought Willard, like bodyguards in a film. The door revolved again and another figure entered the hall – a tall woman, who paused for a moment to take in the scene.

Roo gasped.

Ed's jaw slackened.

Willard made a surprised noise that sounded a bit like 'Oobah!'

'I wasn't expecting you, madam,' said the senior policeman, hurrying over to the newcomer and saluting deferentially. 'This lady,' he said, turning to the others, 'is the Head of the International Art Crime Unit. Her name is—'

'Miss Rosanna Filey,' said Miss Filey. 'And my goodness, I seem to have arrived just in time.'

CHAPTER 27

Despite being Head of the International Art Crime Unit, Miss Filey looked no different to the last time they'd seen her, except that she'd apparently borrowed a raincoat from somebody, to which a large, silver shield-shaped badge had been pinned.

'So, shall I summarize what's happened?' she asked.

'But we haven't told you anything yet,' said the senior policeman.

'I think I can take a jolly good guess,' she said. 'Before that, though, I need to say hello to Mr Hastings and Mr Valentine, whom I last saw receiving their joint "Most Enthusiastic Gallery-Visitor of the Year" prize at the Art Awards Ceremony.' She waved at Coat

Man and Moustache, who waved back. 'And gosh!' she exclaimed, spotting the children, 'my very good friends, Lucy, Willard and Ed are here as well. Oh – and Attlee,' she added, spotting him padding towards the group.

'I had no idea they were friends of yours,' said the policeman. 'But I'm afraid that the young lady's in a great deal of trouble. She removed a picture from its frame.'

'I did *not*!' said Roo.

'I'm jolly well certain she didn't,' said Miss Filey, 'because over there, holding that absolutely super Matisse valued at an enormous amount of money is the notorious art thief Elizabeth de Vere, who always poses as an elderly curator before she carries out her crimes, and who is wanted by the police in eight countries.'

Mabel Collins let out a snarl, turned to run and immediately fell over Attlee, letting go of the goldfish canvas as she did so. It flew through the air and was caught, one-handed, by Ed.

'Good save!' shouted Willard.

'Ow,' said Attlee.

Roo crouched to give him a stroke, while the policeman snapped a pair of handcuffs on a struggling

Mabel Collins, whose white wig had fallen off to reveal brown curls.

'I'll be recommending a medal for these children,' he said, leading his captive away.

'Yessssssssss!' said Willard. 'Do we get anything else though, like a sniffer dog?'

'Or a place on one of those police driving courses,' said Ed absently. He was staring at the picture he was still holding. The goldfish were just two eye-shaped orange blobs in close-up, and yet from a distance, they'd looked real enough to shiver the water of their painted aquarium. It was almost another sort of magic, he thought, and then he looked up again and the whole gallery was swaying gently, the ceiling sinking, the pictures sliding down the walls. 'Take this,' he said hastily, passing the canvas to Coat Man, just as a flowered carpet began to spread across the marble floor like a tide coming in. And the walls drew closer and they were back in the living room – the one with a sofa that wasn't a charred wreck, and a wireless instead of a TV – and this time, Miss Filey was with them.

'We've found you!' Ed exclaimed, as if he'd only just realized. 'We saw you'd been in the rocket.'

'Yes, wasn't it terrific!' said Miss Filey.

'And on the film set,' said Roo.

'And in the boat,' added Willard. He was slightly amazed at how cheerful Miss Filey looked, as if she'd just had a nice afternoon in a teashop rather than being bounced from one bizarre world to another. She was actually beaming.

'Gosh, I had no idea you were looking for me,' she said. 'And Attlee's here too!'

'I was given absolutely no choice in the matter,' said Attlee, who had recovered enough to resume eating a Happee Kittee Prawn-Flavoured Bic that he'd found on the carpet.

'It's all been so extraordinary,' continued Miss Filey. 'I made my wish, and I found myself in my very own zoo, and a tiger had just escaped and it was all terribly thrilling, but it was over awfully quickly and then – I've no idea why – instead of coming back to you, I came *here*. And started having even *more* adventures. I don't know if you realized, but this is my house when I was a little girl, when I was given those birthday candles.' She picked up Attlee and put him gently on the sofa, and then sank down next to him with a sigh of what sounded like happiness. 'Of course, you might not have noticed,' she added, 'because the living room has hardly changed at all since then.'

Attlee gave a sardonic 'Ha!' and the children looked

at each other. 'I'm afraid it's changed a bit more than you'd think,' said Ed unhappily.

'We're really sorry,' said Roo.

'Yes, *really* sorry,' added Willard. And, hesitantly, they told Miss Filey the story of the table and the fire, and the tin of candles. She listened intently, her eyes growing wider and rounder.

'So all five candles melted together?'

'Yes.'

'And the sofa's ruined?'

'Yes.'

'And the whole house absolutely reeks of smoke?'

'Yes.'

'And instead of one short little wish that ended before the story could really get going, I've had four tremendous adventures, and one still to go?'

'Yes.'

'Well, what a *stroke* of luck it was, then!'

'So you honestly don't mind?' asked Willard, trying to imagine what his mum would have said if he'd carelessly set fire to the living room.

'Gosh no, it's only a sofa.'

'Well, *I* mind,' said Attlee. 'That was my favourite spot. But clearly in the scheme of things, my own comfort comes *right* at the bottom of the pile, "Oh look, there's a cat who's the equivalent of a hundred and twenty-five years old, desperately attempting to relax on an enormous heap of charcoal".'

'Oh *no*!' said Ed.

'Well, I'm glad at least one of you is remorseful.'

'No,' said Ed. 'I didn't mean "Oh no" about your sofa – I mean, "Oh no, I've just realized something".' He felt as if his stomach had been hollowed out. 'I've just realized something terrible.' Everyone looked at him; he took a deep breath. 'I dropped the book,' he said. 'When I caught the painting, I dropped the book. I must have left it there. It's gone.'

CHAPTER 28

'Which book did you leave behind?' asked Miss Filey.

'*Your* book – *Adventure Stories for Girls* – the book that all the wishes came from. If we hadn't taken it with us we'd never have known how to escape the comet.'

'Or get past the rocks, or open the treasure box,' said Willard.

'Oh heavens, don't worry,' said Miss Filey. 'I know all those stories almost by heart. And anyway, I'd changed quite a few of them.'

'What do you mean?' asked Ed.

'Well, I sometimes used to alter them in my head, to make them more interesting. For instance, I remember thinking that sailing the boat by myself might be lonely, so I thought it would be rather splendid if I were joined by a friendly seal.'

'The seal!' said Willard. 'Except he *wasn't* very friendly.'

'Oh, you just had to tickle him under the chin. And at the art gallery, I'd wondered if it would be more exciting if the thief was somebody no one would suspect, rather than somebody who looked suspicious in the first place.' She fingered the badge that was still pinned to her raincoat. 'I hadn't realized that I could bring something back from a wish, but I'm rather glad to have this.'

Willard thought of the gold shell in his pocket, and decided he ought to change the subject. 'So . . . where do we go next?' he asked. 'If there's only one more wish left, we should pick something really incredibubble.'

'I think Miss Filey should choose where to go,' said Roo.

'Gosh, I do wish you'd all call me Rosanna. Calling me Miss Filey makes me feel *ancient*.' She grinned as she said it, and the grin made her – for just a second – look ten years old. 'But I think we should all choose together,' she added. 'Let me work out which wishes are left.'

She walked into the hall and the others followed.

'First of all, there's the spare room,' she said, pointing to a closed door along the corridor. 'The bed in there has a white counterpane which always used to make me think of snow, so that's where I imagined the story about an avalanche. "Sally to the Rescue", it was called in the book – she has a Pyrenean mountain dog and she's a champion skier.'

'That sounds good,' said Willard.

'No, I wouldn't like that,' said Roo quickly.

Ed said nothing.

'And next to that room is the linen cupboard, where we kept sheets and towels on shelves. It doesn't have any windows, so it reminded me of the cave in "Rhoda and the Underground Mystery" – I'd imagine climbing down through a series of narrow passages and finding a vast cavern full of paintings that no one had ever found before.'

'No,' said Roo firmly. 'I'd be too scared to do that.'

'You haven't been scared about anything else,' said Willard.

Miss Filey was still talking, her head tilted back as she looked at the ceiling of the hall, where a square hatch was visible. 'And then there's the loft, though it's rather hard to get into – I'd need to get the stepladder from the shed – but I imagined that was the castle under siege where a medieval girl called Aelred gets trapped in a—'

'*No*,' said Roo sharply. 'I don't want to do that either.'

'You OK?' asked Willard. Even Miss Filey had stopped talking and was looking at her rather worriedly.

'I just don't *want* to.' Roo had folded her arms, and her expression was uncomfortable and defiant, nothing like the way that she normally looked.

After a moment, Ed reached out and touched her elbow. 'It's all right, Roo,' he said quietly. 'You don't have to do this.'

'She doesn't have to *what*?' asked Willard.

Ed took a deep breath. 'My sister is trying to pretend that she doesn't want to do any of those wishes, so that *I* don't have to say anything.'

'Oh, gosh,' said Miss Filey, getting it.

'Say anything about what?' asked Willard, not getting it.

'About the fact that I hate being in snow because I can't use my chair properly, and I wouldn't be any good at climbing through caves, and it would need at least two other people to get me up a stepladder. I mean, I know everyone in a wheelchair's supposed to have super-strength or be in the Paralympics or something, but I happen to be better at—'

'Thinking,' said Roo.

'Honesty,' said Miss Filey.

'Sarcasm,' said Willard. '*And* sailing.'

Ed managed a grin. 'I'll take those,' he said. 'Anyway, thanks, sis.'

'That's OK,' said Roo, a bit startled, because Ed was suddenly talking to her as if she was his own age, instead of the way he usually did. 'You're welcome,' she added.

'Just in case anyone was going to ask – which I very much suspect they weren't,' said Attlee, 'none of those wishing options appealed to me either. Given that this time we appear to have an actual *choice*, rather than being *thrust* into the unknown, what else is on offer?'

Miss Filey paused and thought. 'There was one about diving to an undersea wreck,' she said.

'*No*,' said Attlee firmly. 'Is that the lot?'

'No, there was one more: a special wish, that wasn't actually a story in the book – a wish that I made up myself . . .'

'*Everywhere!*' said Roo. 'Was that what the wish was called?'

Miss Filey nodded.

'How do you know that?' asked Willard.

'It was on the end of Miss Filey's . . . I mean, on the end of *Rosanna's* list in the book.'

'Everywhere,' repeated Ed, cautiously repeating the word as if it was a jellybean that might taste either of strawberries or earwax. 'But how can a wish be "Everywhere"?'

'And which room is it in?' asked Willard.

'It's in my parents' room.' Rosanna walked to the door at the end of the corridor, and the others followed her.

'When my mother first came home from hospital,' said Rosanna, 'this was where she spent most of her days. She couldn't leave the house to see the world, so I used to dream about bringing the world to her. I wished she could see all the places that I'd read about, all the names I'd picked out on the globe, all the super things I was going to see and do when I was older.'

'I'm up for that,' said Willard.

'I'm afraid I require just a smidgeon more detail,' said Attlee. 'How, precisely, would that work? Could one, for instance, experience "everywhere" while seated on a comfortable chair, sheltered from unnecessary draughts?'

'Yes, because that's exactly what I imagined for my mother. Shall I show you?' asked Rosanna.

Roo looked at Ed. *'What do you think?'* she mouthed.

And Ed, who secretly thought that Attlee had a point, saw the excitement flowering on his sister's face, and managed a nod. 'Sounds good,' he said. 'Let's go.'

CHAPTER 29

It was a comfortable, welcoming room, with a double bed covered by a patchwork quilt in shades of blue and violet, and a squashy blue velvet armchair; a woollen shawl was folded over one of the arms. The large window looked out onto the back garden, and a rectangular patch of sunlight lay across the chair and the bedside table. There was a globe on the table – the globe that had stood on the desk in Rosanna's library; it had been faded then, but it was bright and new now, the north and south poles shining white, the continents mottled with green and brown and orange, the seas a vivid blue.

'It's nice in here,' said Roo.

Attlee stood beside the armchair, staring fixedly. She lifted him onto the seat and he settled down with a sigh and closed his eyes. 'If anything exciting should happen,' he said, '*please* don't wake me. So far today, I have been weightless, trapped, ignored, starved, dropped, abandoned and tripped over and now I require a good long sleep. Having said that' – he opened his eyes again – 'I'd like to take this opportunity to confirm the truth of the compliment that I paid you earlier today.'

'You paid me a compliment?' asked Roo, amazed.

'I believe that I said you were more intelligent than you look.'

'That's *definitely* not a compliment,' said Ed, but Roo took the shawl and tucked it around Attlee, and after a moment she heard, for the first time, the throaty buzz of his purr.

'I think,' said Rosanna, who had gone over to the globe and was gently wiping a trace of dust from Alaska, 'that Attlee likes you far more than he likes me. I think he simply regards me as—'

The door of the room slammed shut. Willard gave a little bounce of excitement. 'Here comes Everywhere!' he said, and as he spoke, he saw a movement out of the corner of his eye; the globe had started to revolve, slowly but steadily.

'What happens now?' asked Ed, wheeling towards it.

'I imagined I'd choose a place,' said Rosanna, 'and dab my finger exactly onto it, and then . . . we'd be there.'

The four of them stared at the spinning globe.

'What's that little bright thing?' asked Roo, as a flash of silver went past.

'The head of a pin,' said Rosanna. 'I put it in to mark this house. I planned that when I grew up and started travelling, I'd put a different-coloured pin into every place I visited.'

The globe continued to turn; there were no other pins.

Willard reached out a tentative finger in the direction of the USA and then withdrew it. 'You should go first,' he said to Rosanna.

'Or how about youngest first?' she asked, looking at Roo.

'All right,' said Roo. 'I think I know where I want to go.' She leaned forward and looked intently at the countries moving smoothly by: Japan . . . India . . . Egypt . . . Greece . . . Then she saw the name of the place that she wanted, and carefully dabbed a finger at the globe . . .

. . . and they were there. Or they were *somewhere*. 'Oh,' said Roo, disconcerted.

It was raining and she was in the middle of a field, together with Ed, Rosanna, Willard, the armchair (containing Attlee) and the chest of drawers, on which the globe was still spinning.

The field was dull, flat and boggy and beyond the wire fence on all sides were more fields, also dull, flat and boggy. From the distance came a faint mooing. From close by came the strong smell of cow poo.

'Where are we?' asked Willard, holding his nose and looking down at his trainers, which were sinking into the ooze. As were Ed's wheels.

'Scotland,' said Roo disappointedly. 'I always wanted to go to Scotland. But I thought it would be more like your postcard,' she said to Ed. 'The one you sent when you went on the sailing course.'

'What did it show?' asked Ed, hunching his shoulders to stop the rain dripping down the back of his neck.

'It had lots of little pictures on it – a beautiful lake and mountains and the sun and a golden eagle and some deer and purple heather and things. I thought all of Scotland would be like that.'

'Well, they wouldn't sell many postcards if they photographed this bit,' said Ed.

'Still, it's very . . .' Rosanna looked around, as if searching for something to praise. '*Fresh*,' she added kindly. 'Let's all breathe in the lovely country air.'

There was a snore from Attlee.

'Can we do my choice now?' asked Willard, still holding his nose. 'Unless you want to stay longer, Roo?'

'No, it's OK.'

'Oh, please let's stay longer,' said Ed. 'And then we could go to the fence and back a couple of times. Or play "guess the number of cowpats".'

'Sometimes you sound just like Attlee,' said Willard.

'No, I don't,' said Ed indignantly.

Roo was still gazing round. 'I think I should've gone for something more . . . what's that word?'

'Dry,' said Willard.

'Specific?' suggested Ed.

'Yes, specific.'

'*My* choice is definitely specific,' said Willard. 'I know exactly where it is because I've looked it up on Google Earth at least a hundred times. *And* it's usually dry and sunny there.'

'Splendid,' said Rosanna.

'Shall I do it then?'

'Yes,' said Ed.

'Right.' Willard splashed over to the chest of drawers and focused on the spinning globe, his finger poised. 'OK, everybody,' he said, his voice tight with anticipation. 'We're all going to . . . *Disney World*!!'

His finger landed on the 'A' of FLORIDA.

And suddenly there was screaming.

CHAPTER 30

'Woah!' exclaimed Willard. The air was as hot as if they were standing in front of a hair-dryer, and from somewhere very close by, they could hear the deafening, distinctive noise of a thunderous roller coaster full of yelling passengers.

'We must be here,' shouted Willard. 'I did it!!'

'Oh, jolly well done!' said Rosanna.

'We might be in Disney World, but *where* are we?' asked Ed, looking round. 'I mean, what are we standing in?'

The four of them – together with Attlee's chair and the chest of drawers – seemed to be in a sort of tunnel: a short, flat-floored, square-sided concrete tunnel, open to a fierce blue sky at both ends. On one side of the tunnel was a blank wall, but on the other, at about the level of Rosanna's shoulders, was a row of large metal rectangles.

Screaming began again, and they heard the roller coaster whoosh past in the other direction.

'It couldn't come through this tunnel, could it?' asked Roo anxiously.

'No, there's no track,' said Ed, looking down at the smooth floor. 'Don't worry.'

'It really is rather a peculiar place,' said Rosanna, looking up at the ceiling.

'I wonder which roller coaster we can hear?' asked Willard. 'It might be that one that goes through water, or the one that goes underground or the one that—' His voice was drowned out by more screaming, this time passing above them.

'Let's go and see,' said Ed. He set out towards the nearest end of the tunnel and the others followed. The view opened out as they approached; great loops and spirals of roller coaster track became visible, and as they reached the knee-high guard rail at the end, they realized that they were quite high up. Beneath them were crowds of people and a mass of spinning, whirling, roaring rides.

The screams began again, and this time they could actually see the roller coaster passengers, mouths opened in joyous terror as they rocketed around the circuit, swaying beneath the track, shooting out sideways as they went round the tight corners.

'Oh, it's an *inverted* roller coaster,' said Willard knowledgeably. 'It's called that when you hang *underneath* the track, instead of riding on the top. I think this is the world's longest because it goes round twice and it—'

'Gosh, sorry to interrupt,' said Rosanna, 'but does that explain what this is?'

'What *what* is?' asked Willard.

Rosanna pointed upward.

Directly above them and stretching along the whole length of the tunnel ceiling, was a roller coaster track.

'Oh,' said Roo, in a tiny voice. 'It *does* go through here, then.'

Ed was already spinning round. 'Those metal things on the wall are *doors*. This tunnel's where the people get off and on.'

'Or not!' shouted Willard. 'If it goes round twice.' Looking outward again, he could see the riders looping the loop, and his gaze zipped along the track ahead of them. There was a corkscrew, a climb, and then a sudden, steep turn which ended at *the exact place where they were standing.* 'I think we've got about thirty seconds before they get here,' he said.

'We need to skedaddle,' said Rosanna firmly, holding out a hand to Roo.

'Need to *what*?' asked Willard.

'To get going,' shouted Ed, who was already scooting back along the tunnel to where Attlee was still sleeping. 'Or we'll be swept out or knocked down or squashed flat.' He reached the still-spinning globe just ahead of the others.

'Where should we go?' he shouted, over his shoulder.

'Anywhere,' called Rosanna and Roo simultaneously.

'Can you try Disneyland California?' suggested Willard, turning back to see the square blue hole of the tunnel end. It was suddenly, deafeningly, full of dangling, screaming passengers. 'DO IT!!!' he yelled.

Ed peered at the globe, saw a familiar word and jabbed his finger at it . . .

. . . and they were in the middle of a dull, flat and boggy field. It was raining.

'Scotland?' asked Willard.

'Yup,' said Ed. 'It seemed the safest option. Though I was sort of trying to aim for the Glasgow Science

Centre, where we went on the way home from the sailing course. I missed, obviously.'

'Right,' said Willard. 'Woah,' he added, still a bit breathless. Everyone was looking slightly wobbly and wide-eyed.

'Good *Lord*, that was close!' exclaimed Rosanna. 'Golly gosh. I can see, now, that I didn't plan this wish terribly well. It lacks . . .'

'Precision?' suggested Ed.

'Yes.'

There was a faint baaing in the distance.

'It's definitely not the same field,' said Roo, who'd been looking around with interest. 'The last one had a metal gate, and this one's got a wooden one.'

'And it doesn't smell as much,' said Willard.

'That's because the last one had cow poo,' said Ed, 'and this one has *sheep* poo.'

The rain seemed to be getting slightly heavier. Rosanna bent over to peer at the globe. Roo checked on Attlee, but he was still snoring contentedly beneath the shawl.

'So, should we go home now, maybe?' she asked, a bit hopefully. It seemed a really long time since she'd been in an ordinary place, doing ordinary things, and she couldn't help imagining how nice it would be to sit and watch telly for half an hour, while eating spaghetti on toast.

'Rosanna hasn't had a go yet,' said Willard. 'And it's *her* wish, after all.'

'That's true,' said Ed, who was starting to get extremely tired of the ceaseless trickle of rain down the back of his neck.

'Shall I?' asked Rosanna, looking round at them; Ed could see the eagerness in her expression.

'Go for it,' he said.

'Very well. How about . . .' She hovered a finger over the Indian Ocean as it slowly turned 'Madagascar? Or maybe somewhere more mountainous, so we have a view . . .' Her finger drifted southwest. 'Lesotho, perhaps? Or the Rockies . . .' Her finger crossed the Atlantic 'Or maybe Chile?' And at that moment, just as her finger was whizzing down the spine of South America, Attlee sneezed violently and unexpectedly, and Rosanna jumped.

'Oops,' said Willard.

CHAPTER 31

'Where are we?' shouted Roo into a fierce wind that snatched the words away as soon as they left her mouth. Ed shook his head and gaped round at a view that was so vast and wild that for once he could find nothing to say.

They were bunched together on a plateau of bare rock; above them, clouds galloped across a cold blue sky. Behind them, the ground rose steeply towards a cluster of savage peaks, patterned with glittering ice; in front of them, and on either side, the rock sloped down to the sea, where waves as high as houses pounded a beach of black sand. The sea was a dark, dark blue and it glinted like a sheet of foil. The only sounds were the relentless roar of wind and water and the high cry of seabirds. There wasn't a single human sign – not a ship or a shop or a fence or a road. He had never been anywhere so empty. He had never felt so small.

'WHERE ARE WE?' repeated Roo. A sudden gust sent her staggering into Willard, and he grabbed her by one arm, and held onto Ed's chair with the other.

There was a crash as the chest of drawers blew over. Behind it stood Rosanna, clutching the base of the globe. The top part was spinning so fast in the wind that the continents were just a green blur.

'I'm fearfully sorry!' she shouted. 'I didn't actually mean to come here. Attlee made me jump and I'm afraid my finger hit the wrong place.'

'Oh, so it's all *my* fault?' said a waspish voice from under the shawl on the armchair. 'I hadn't realized.'

'But where's *here*?' yelled Willard.

'I think we're in Tierra del Fuego!' shouted Rosanna, carefully separating and projecting each word, so that they could almost read her lips. 'The southernmost tip of South America, where the Pacific and the Atlantic meet. It's one of the wildest places on Earth, with some of the worst weather. It's rather splendid, isn't it?' And though her hair was blowing sideways and her knuckles were blue with cold, the most noticeable thing about her, Ed realized with surprise, was that she looked absolutely *thrilled*.

The clouds were thickening and the sky began to darken. Something stung Ed's face and he realized that there was snow in the wind, small hard flakes that felt as if someone was throwing grit at him.

There was another gust of wind, and the shawl blew off the armchair and wrapped itself round Willard's head.

'I distinctly remember . . .' said Attlee, raising his voice, his claws desperately gripping the seat, the wind parting his fur as if it were a field of grass, '. . . I distinctly remember using the phrase "sheltered from unnecessary draughts".'

As he spoke there was a flickering in the sky and three colossal bolts of lightning leaped from the heavy cloud. Two prodded the sea and one struck the rising ground behind them.

For a second the light was as white and as brilliant as a flashbulb, and then it was back to gloom again, and a smell of fireworks.

'My fault, obviously!' called Attlee. 'Apologies to everyone concerned.'

'In my last school we had a lesson on what to do

in a—' began Willard, before being drowned out by a clap of thunder.

'. . . so if there's lightning, you mustn't stand under a tree,' continued Willard.

'There aren't any trees,' shouted Roo.

'Or touch anything metal,' said Willard. 'Oh,' he added, looking at Ed's wheelchair.

Ed raised his voice. 'We have to get out of here!'

'Yes, I think you're probably right,' said Miss Filey, sounding rather reluctant.

Another spoke of lightning hit the rocky slopes behind them.

'Sorry, everybody,' called Attlee.

The wind gusted again and the globe seemed to whirl even faster. 'But how do we choose a place?' asked Roo. 'We can't read any of the names any more.'

'We could just, you know, point *anywhere*,' said Willard.

'NO,' shouted Ed. 'That's too dangerous. What if we ended up in the middle of the Pacific or something?'

'Well, you could simply blame *me* for it,' said Attlee.

As he spoke, lightning struck again, and for a fraction of a second, something flashed brightly on the spinning globe.

'The pin!' called Rosanna. 'The pin I put in to mark my house! If we could touch that, we'd be home.'

'But how can we?' asked Ed. 'It's going too fast.'

'It's like something you have to do in a video game except I don't think we'd get another go,' said Willard, peering at the globe.

'I know who could do it,' called Roo. 'Remember when Attlee took that jigsaw piece out of the box – he did it so quickly I didn't see his paw move.'

'That's right!' said Ed. 'He picked out one particular piece in, like, a nanosecond. Attlee can do it!'

'Oh, Attlee can do it, can he?' said Attlee. 'Have you even *asked* him?'

Roo pushed through the wind to where Attlee lay on the chair, looking frozen and furious. She knelt and stroked his head. 'Please,' she said.

'Please!' shouted Willard.

'Please,' said Ed.

'Please, dear old fellow,' called Rosanna. 'You're the only one who can get us out of this fix.'

Attlee raised his head. 'Lift me up,' he commanded Roo.

'*Please*,' shouted Willard reprovingly. Attlee ignored him.

Roo picked him up and held him in front of the whirling globe and he stared at it unblinkingly. To Roo's eyes, the pin was almost invisible. Attlee shifted slightly in her arms. There was another flash of lightning, the pin head lit up like a torch, Attlee's paw was a sudden blur – and the doorbell rang.

The doorbell rang!

They were back! They were back in the bedroom and the still, quiet air was like the touch of a velvet blanket.

'Oh, I say, well done, Attlee,' said Rosanna, stooping to put the globe on the floor. It was still spinning, but more slowly now.

'Three cheers for Attlee!' shouted Willard.

'You were brilliant,' said Ed. 'Thank you.'

Attlee blinked modestly.

Roo lowered him onto the chair again, and Willard gave her the shawl back. Attlee was shivering slightly, and she carefully covered him up.

The doorbell rang again.

'I suppose we should answer that,' said Rosanna, attempting to smooth down her hair. Like all of them, she looked as if she'd just been through the spin cycle in a washing machine.

'I'll go,' said Ed. 'It's my turn.' He opened the bedroom door, and behind him Roo gave a gasp.

'What's the matter?' asked Ed.

'The globe's stopped spinning – and that was the final wish, wasn't it? Do you think that means we're back? I mean, back *now*.'

There was a pause. 'I can smell smoke,' said Rosanna.

'We're back,' said Ed.

CHAPTER 32

The doorbell rang for the third time just before Ed opened the door. It was his father.

'Oh, there you are,' he said, blinking slightly at Ed's windswept appearance. 'It's just that your mum and I were expecting you for tea about an hour ago.'

'Oh, sorry,' said Ed. 'We were . . . busy.'

'I can still smell smoke,' said his father. 'It's very *strong*. Not like burned toast at all.'

'Yes, we were . . .' Ed racked his brains for a believable answer.

'Oh, hello, Mr Crane,' said Rosanna, from over Ed's shoulder. 'The children were just very kindly helping me to . . . to . . . set fire to a sofa.'

'Set fire to a sofa?' asked Ed's dad, looking a bit stunned. 'Why?'

There was a pause.

'It was old!' shouted Willard from behind them.

'Yes, it was old,' agreed Rosanna. 'So, I asked them to drag it out to the garden for me and then we . . .'

'Incinerated it,' said Ed.

'OK,' said Ed's dad hesitantly. 'So, er, are you coming back for tea now?'

'Can we come in ten minutes?' asked Ed. 'We've got to . . . you know . . .' He couldn't think of anything.

'Tidy up,' shouted Roo, from the hall.

'Yes, we've got to tidy everything up, so it all looks nice,' agreed Ed.

If anything, this sentence made his father look even more stunned than before. 'OK,' he said uncertainly. 'We'll see you in ten minutes, then.'

'Bye, Dad,' said Ed. He backed up and closed the door and turned round to the others. Rosanna's mouth was bunched up and she was making an odd noise; it took him a moment to realize that she was giggling. And so was Roo. And so was Willard, who pointed a wavering finger at Rosanna. '*The children were very kindly helping me to set fire to a sofa,*' he quoted, between gasps.

Ed started laughing too. 'Yes, Furniture Cremation,' he said. 'Always top of the list of "How To Entertain Your Neighbours' Kids at Half Term".' Rosanna let out a sort of shriek and covered her mouth with a hand.

'And you, Ed,' said Roo, her voice wobbling, '"*We've got to tidy everything up, so it all looks nice.*" Dad nearly fainted.'

'Oh, heavens,' said Rosanna, taking out a handkerchief and wiping her eyes. 'I haven't laughed like that for . . . gosh . . . ages and ages. And what a day. What a day!'

'*Should* we tidy up?' asked Ed. 'I mean, can we help you?'

'No, not at all. I'm going to throw an old sheet over the sofa, and phone the council tomorrow to take it away. I think probably the only person who'll miss it will be Attlee and – oh, perhaps we'd better check on him again. He did look rather cold.'

They went back to the bedroom. Attlee was still curled up on the armchair, covered with the shawl.

'Attlee, are you all right?' asked Rosanna. There was no movement from beneath the shawl.

A couple of seconds went by.

'Attlee?' repeated Rosanna more quietly.

All was still.

'He said before we went on the adventure he wanted a good long sleep,' said Roo. 'Didn't he?'

Willard nudged Ed and pulled a face of dread.

'Hey, Roo,' said Ed. 'Let's leave him alone, shall we?'

'Why?'

'I think Ed's right,' said Rosanna softly. 'Perhaps we should let him sleep. He's had a very busy day.'

They all looked at the lump on the armchair.

'But . . .' Roo looked from Ed to Rosanna and back again. 'You're not saying that . . .'

There was a sudden movement beneath the shawl and Attlee reared up, opened his mouth, made a really disgusting retching noise and coughed up a hairball, before settling back down again with some contented groans.

'How lovely,' said Ed.

Tenderly, Roo covered him up again, and they all went back into the hall. For a moment, nobody spoke.

'I suppose me and Roo should go home,' said Ed. It seemed a very ordinary end to the most extraordinary day of his life. 'Thanks and everything.'

'Thank *you*, Ed,' said Rosanna. 'And thank you, Lucy.'

'I ought to go home too or my mum'll be worried,' said Willard. 'Can I climb over your back wall?'

'Of course,' said Rosanna.

'OK.' Willard stuck out a hand and Rosanna shook it. 'See you around, then,' he said.

'Yes, indeed.'

'See you, Ed. See you, Luce.' He gave a wave and went into the living room. 'Stinks in here!' they heard him say, before the sound of the French windows being opened.

'Can I just get Attlee something to eat before we go?' said Roo. 'I think there were some of those prawn bics left.' She went off to fetch the packet, and a bowl.

The house seemed suddenly incredibly quiet.

'You could put some more pins in the globe now,' said Ed, after a pause.

'Yes, I suppose I could,' said Rosanna. 'Though that might be a bit of a cheat; I'd say you actually have to *travel* to a destination before it truly counts.'

'Well, you could do that as well, couldn't you?'

'Travel, you mean? Oh, gosh . . .' Rosanna looked down at her hands, at the freckly skin and shiny knuckles. 'No, I think it's probably a bit too late for all that. It was a super wish, all the same,' she added quietly.

Ed frowned. 'But you shouldn't—'

'All done!' announced Roo, skipping back. 'Attlee seems quite hungry, though of course he can't talk any more.'

'Oh, what a pity,' said Ed sarcastically, and then paused. 'You don't really think I sound like him, do you?'

'Oh no, *never*,' said Roo, equally sarcastically and he gave her a reluctant grin.

'I suppose we'd better go,' Roo added, and she darted forward and wrapped her arms around Rosanna's waist. 'Thank you.'

'Oh gosh, Lucy, you're welcome. You're both welcome.' She smiled at Ed over the top of Roo's head.

And then they went home, and that was that.

Except it wasn't.

CHAPTER 33

That night, Willard couldn't sleep. At half past midnight, he got up and switched on the light, and took the gold shell from where he'd hidden it inside a football sock.

'Why are you Googling gold prices?' his mother had asked earlier when she'd brought him a mug of hot chocolate.

'I was . . . I was thinking about pirate treasure,' he'd said, which was almost true. 'I read a story about it,' he added, which wasn't. 'Did you know that gold sells at fifty pounds *a gram*?'

'Oh, you've been *reading*!' his mother had said happily.

Just before bedtime, he'd secretly borrowed the kitchen scales and had weighed the shell, and had then used a calculator to work out how much it was worth. The result had been so unbelievable that he'd checked it twice, to make sure.

Now he sat on his bed, holding the heavy object in his hand, wondering about all the things he could buy if he sold it. And about how he would explain to his mum that he had suddenly acquired a fantastically valuable antique, and whether it was really his in the first place, and also whether arriving at a new school on a platinum skateboard would actually make things easier for him, or even harder. And then he thought, with a nudge of happiness, that at least this time he already knew people at the school – he had *friends* there and he'd never really had a friend like Ed before: someone smart and a bit spiky who made jokes of his own, and who sometimes even laughed at Willard's . . .

An idea began to form in his head and, grinning, he got up to put the shell away again and saw a crescent moon edging round the window frame, and instead of customized skateboards he started thinking instead of the glorious, stomach-twirling sensation of weightlessness, and of how the moon had filled half the sky, its craters like dark thumbprints on a china plate, and he went over to the shelf by the window and took out the book on space exploration that his gran had bought him for Christmas two years ago. He'd never opened it before.

Roo was lying awake as well. Too much had happened; too many extraordinary images were still swirling inside her head – if she closed her eyes, it was like watching a fairground ride. She opened them again; the streetlight outside was shining through a crack in the curtains and sending a small wedge of yellow light across the ceiling. It looked a bit like a candle flame. Maybe, thought Roo, if she were to list all the wishes, it might send her to sleep.

One, she thought, *the dog. Two, the tame ant. Three, the aeroplane. Four, Attlee talking. Five, Miss Filey's wish. Six* . . .

She frowned. Something wasn't quite right; something was missing from the list. She went back over it and remembered the little extra wish that Willard had made with the leftover candle stub, after Ed had blown it out. She started again. *One, the dog. Two, the tame ant* and *Willard becoming a millionaire. Three, the aeroplane. Four, Attlee talking, Five* . . .

No, she thought, it still wasn't right. There was still

something missing. Something small. Something very, very small . . .

Ed couldn't sleep either. His brain felt like a box of bees, but the biggest bee of all, the one that kept banging against the inside of his skull, was the memory of his last conversation with Miss Filey. When the sky at last began to lighten, he gave up trying to sleep and quietly got dressed and went downstairs on his bum, one step at a time, to where his wheelchair was parked in the hall.

In the living room, the builders had blocked the gap in the wall with a temporary wooden panel, so the room looked a bit like a shed. Ed went to the kitchen, put a slice of bread in the toaster, poured himself some cereal, and opened the back door; in the spot where his new bedroom was supposed to be, there was a large, muddy hole. It had been fenced off, but he could just glimpse the smashed stonework of the well which the builders had discovered, and which had meant that work had had to stop. He closed the door again and went over to the fridge, edging round the table that took up most of the kitchen space.

The house felt very cramped. At Rosanna's, the large square rooms and wide corridor meant that he could zoom around, but here he had to brake and manoeuvre all the time – it was like a slalom course, a constant reminder that he couldn't walk any more.

'You're up early,' said his dad, coming into the kitchen, wearing the boring grey shirt and black trousers he always wore when he was giving a driving lesson. 'Any plans for the day?'

'Not really. Though I need to go back and see Rosanna.'

'Who's Rosanna?'

'Miss Filey. She told us to call her that,' he added quickly, when his dad looked startled. 'I need to talk to her about something.'

'Don't, um . . .' His father hesitated.

'What?'

'Burn any more of her furniture, will you? Even if she asks.'

'I won't,' said Ed. 'I promise.'

It was still early when Ed arrived at the house, but as he hesitated at the gate, the front door opened and Rosanna came out, holding a bucket and sponge and a pair of rubber gloves.

'Oh, I was just about to wash out the dustbin,' she said, 'but gosh, I'd much rather see you! Do come in.'

He followed her into the hall. It was so strange to think that just a few days ago, he'd arrived at this exact spot, certain that he was just about to have the dullest week of his life in the dullest house he'd ever visited, and now every object and every door seemed to shout out to him, like old friends. And the kindly, awkward woman that he'd laughed at (and who had just this minute started to ask him about whether he wanted biscuits or cake) had become an old friend too.

'I wanted to say something,' he said abruptly.

Rosanna must have read something in his expression, because she stopped talking, put down the bucket and sponge and gloves and sat down at the telephone table. 'Go on,' she said, and Ed had the sudden, odd feeling that *he* was the grown-up and she was the child. He took a deep breath; what he needed to say was important, and he had to make it clear.

'Yesterday, you said that it was probably too late for you to go travelling.'

She nodded.

'It's not,' he said. 'Go now.'

'Now?'

'Yes. All those places are still there, waiting for you. And so are all those people you write to, but you've never visited. What's stopping you?'

'Gosh. I'm not . . .' Rosanna looked all around the room, as if the answer might be painted on the walls. 'I'm not sure.'

'I mean, when we were in that storm, yesterday, you were enjoying it way more than the rest of us. So why wouldn't you want to travel there for real?'

She looked again at the walls and the ceiling, but this time it was as if she was looking past them, through them, beyond them, to a view that was both wonderful – and frightening. 'I've been here my whole life,' she said rather helplessly. 'It would be such a . . . a jump.'

'Well, I think you should,' said Ed, and though he tried to make his voice firm, he could hear it shake a little. 'Because you don't ever know what's going to happen. Because next month or next year, everything could change, and all the things you thought were average and ordinary and forever might suddenly be difficult, and all the things you thought were difficult might suddenly be impossible and . . . and . . .' His voice dried up for a moment.

Rosanna's eyes were fixed on his. 'And that's something that you know about, isn't it, Ed?' she asked gently.

'Yes,' said Ed, his throat still feeling tight. 'Yes, it's

something I know about. And you don't ever want to think, "Oh, I wish I'd had a go at all that when I had the chance", and . . .' His voice disappeared again, and during the pause, a familiar stench drifted into the room. 'And I can smell Attlee,' he added. He looked around and saw the cat entering the hall from the kitchen, a revolting glob of something that glistened, dangling from one whisker. Attlee threw Ed a dismissive glance and slunk straight past. And then flinched as a very loud knocking came from the living room.

CHAPTER 34

It was Willard, banging his knuckles against the French windows.

'Can I come in?' he called to Rosanna, as she arrived to open them. 'Hi,' he said, seeing Ed. 'You'll never guess what's happened. Hi, Attlee.' There was a pause. 'Forgot he can't speak. Anyway, I have to tell you something really, really weird.'

'You mean, something even more weird than all of us plus a talking cat shooting into outer space in a kitchen?' said Ed.

Willard considered this for a moment. 'OK, not *that* weird. But still . . . listen to this. Just to warn you, it starts off really, really good, but it ends up tragic. You know that treasure chest, the one in the middle of the island? Well, you know the gold shell that was in it? I took it.'

'Took it where?'

'Back with me. In my pocket. I mean, it didn't really belong to anyone, did it? Anyway, I weighed it last night and it's really heavy and it must be worth thousands and thousands and I was thinking about it and I had this idea . . .'

'Technically, I'd say it belonged to Rosanna,' said Ed.

'Oh gosh, that's very nice of you,' said Rosanna, 'but I don't think I could claim something that someone found in a wish.'

'Anyway,' said Willard more loudly, because he was about to say something that really did deserve being listened to – and praised. 'Anyway, I had this idea that we could sell it and divide the money between us all. You two, and me and your sister.'

'Oh!' said Ed. He thought of the new bedroom that might get built onto his house, without having to do any more fundraising. 'Well, that would be . . . brilliant.'

'Yes, really jolly fair-minded of you,' said Rosanna.

Attlee made a retching noise, as if violently disagreeing.

'*But*,' said Willard. 'Something happened. I got up this morning, and I went to the drawer where I'd put it – I mean, I was really careful, it was in a football sock – and it wasn't there, and I thought a burglar must have come in the night and then I turned the sock inside out and these sort of . . . *bits* . . . came out.' He'd kept one of his fists clenched the whole time, and now he opened it. On the palm were a few tiny flakes of gold and a dusting of pearly fragments.

'It's like it totally . . .'

'. . . disintegrated,' finished Ed.

'And then I thought, what happened to that special sick bag I brought back from the flying wish? Do you remember?'

'Yes, but I don't know where it went,' said Ed.

'Oh, the brown paper bag with the picture of an aeroplane on it?' asked Rosanna. 'I put it in my bag drawer. Let's go and have a look.'

Ed and Willard followed her into the kitchen. She opened a drawer and they all peered in. On top of a neatly folded plastic carrier bag were a few tiny specks of brown paper, like the remains of a dried-up autumn leaf.

Ed reached out and pressed a finger onto one of the fragments and held it up to the light. 'Just leftovers,' he said. 'Like when you wake up after a strong dream, and it seems real for hours and hours . . .'

'. . . and then all at once,' continued Rosanna, 'it fades away, and you wonder how you could ever have believed it.'

Nobody spoke. Ed pushed away the vision of the newly-built bedroom, and Willard dusted his hands; for a moment the gold and pearl glittered briefly in the air, then disappeared.

And then the doorbell rang. 'It's me!' shouted a voice through the letter box. 'Please hurry up, I've got something to tell you. Something important!'

'Roo!' said Ed. Willard ran to answer it. Roo was talking even as the door was opening, her words all running together, her face shining with excitement.

'And then – and then' – she took a huge gulp of air – 'and then I rushed all the way here, and Ed's just got to look in the pocket to see if it's still there!' she finished triumphantly, just as the door closed.

'If what's still where?' asked Willard.

'I'm awfully confused,' said Rosanna.

'Start again,' said Ed. 'We missed the beginning. And the middle.'

Roo felt as if she might explode like a firework but she forced herself to repeat the story. 'Last night I couldn't sleep—'

'Me neither,' said Ed and Willard simultaneously.

'And I was lying awake counting up all the wishes in my head, and I kept thinking I'd missed one out, but I couldn't remember what it was. And in the end, I must have fallen asleep because suddenly it was morning, and the answer was' – she banged a finger against her forehead – 'in here. I just *knew*. Do you remember the first candle, the candle where I wished Miss Filey – Rosanna – had a dog? We stuck the candle in a cake.'

'My cake,' said Willard.

'Yes, Willard's cake, and the cake got knocked over and the candle went out. And then we found it later on—'

Attlee made a vomiting noise.

'I mean *Attlee* found it later on, under the sofa.'

'Yes!' shouted Ed. 'And we wrapped it up and put it in' – he was already digging around in the side-pocket on the wheelchair – 'put it in *here*!!!' Triumphantly, he took out what looked like a screwed-up paper towel, and very carefully unwrapped it.

Lying on the crumpled surface was a small silver and white candle.

CHAPTER 35

One more wish.

They had one more wish.

About a third of the candle had already been burned. 'How long do you think we'd get?' asked Willard.

'Maybe three minutes,' said Ed.

'So what should we wish for?'

For a moment, no one spoke.

'I think you should choose,' said Roo to Rosanna. 'They're your candles.'

'I rather think we all should,' said Rosanna. 'What if each of us were to write down an idea, and then we put it to the vote?'

They all nodded, and she went to fetch paper and pencils.

Roo knelt down beside Attlee; she hardly noticed the smell any more.

'Would you like to come too, wherever we go?' she asked.

'He can't speak,' said Willard. 'How about give a miaow for yes—'

'And a vomit for no,' suggested Ed.

Attlee opened his eyes a crack and then sneezed violently.

'What's that?' asked Willard.

'That's "stop teasing me, I'm a hundred and twenty-five years old",' said Roo.

Rosanna came back with the pens and paper, and they went into the dining room and sat around the table. Willard and Roo wrote their answers quickly and folded their bits of paper, but Ed stared at his for a while, frowning, before beginning on what looked like half a page of suggestions.

Rosanna, meanwhile, sat with her eyes closed, her pen gripped tightly, the paper blank. A minute went by. Ed finished writing. Another minute went by, and Rosanna still sat there.

'Are you OK?' asked Roo tentatively.

'What?' Startled, Rosanna opened her eyes. 'Gosh, yes, I'm so sorry. I began by thinking about what I was going to write, but then I rather drifted off onto another topic.'

'Another topic more interesting than choosing an *actual wish*?' asked Willard.

'What was it?' asked Roo.

'Oh, it was . . . something I'd been discussing with Ed, a little earlier.' She directed a shy smile at Ed, and then looked again at her piece of paper. 'I think I'd rather just see your ideas. My head's too full at the moment.'

'You read them out, then,' said Roo.

Rosanna unfolded the first suggestion and gave a gasp. 'It says PROPER FLYING,' she said, sounding thrilled.

'That's mine,' said Willard. 'I mean flying with wings, not an aeroplane.'

Roo bounced in her seat. 'Read mine next,' she said, pushing the slip of paper across the table.

Rosanna opened it. 'FLYING LIKE A BIRD,' she read out.

Wordlessly, Ed offered his own paper.

'Goodness,' said Rosanna, surveying what looked like an essay. 'Here goes.'

I am going to say 'flying' but we need to be quite specific about what sort of flying. If we suddenly get wings, we'd have to start by going outside and then we'd probably use up the whole 3 minutes just learning to flap them. If we choose to become birds, then if we're not careful we might end up as pigeons or something, eating dropped crisps on a pavement, or we could choose to be eagles or hawks, but if we found ourselves soaring very high up, it might feel a bit similar to looking out of a plane window. Anyway I've got an idea and I can't be bothered to write any more, so just ask me.

Rosanna stopped reading and looked at Ed expectantly.

'OK,' he said. 'I've thought about this a lot, ever since we were on that aeroplane. To really, properly feel what it's like to fly, I think we'd have to start off by *not* flying – what I mean is, we'd need to start by launching ourselves from a perch or a branch or something, so we'd get that moment of *suddenly* being airborne.'

Willard, who had been listening intently, gave a

little jerk forward, as if he was jumping from something. 'OK,' he said, 'I get that.'

'And then I had this idea,' continued Ed. 'You know swifts? You know you only ever see them way up in the sky, in summer, just little dark curves, like eyebrows, swooping around? Well, when they first leave the nest, swifts don't flutter to a tree and then spend days learning to fly properly and being fed by their parents – they jump out and that's *it*. The next time they sit down on something is when they get to Africa.'

'Like getting into a car on your first driving lesson and winning a Grand Prix,' said Willard.

'What do they call it?' asked Roo. 'When they jump out of the nest for the first time?'

'Fledging,' said Ed. 'And the young swifts are called fled*glings*, and once fledglings fledge, there's no going back . . .'

They looked at one another; the air seemed to hum with excitement.

'I don't think we need to vote, do we?' asked Rosanna. 'I'll go and get the matches.'

Willard's blob of used chewing gum had disappeared, but Rosanna found a drawing pin and pushed it into the bottom of the candle and then placed the candle on a heavy magnet she used for picking up pins, and then put the magnet in a wide china bowl, on the table.

'Very safe,' said Ed approvingly.

'So, are we ready?'

'Hang on,' said Roo. 'I'm going to check with Attlee.' She left the room and, after a minute returned, carrying the cat.

'He wants to come,' she said.

'How do you *know*?' asked Willard and Ed.

'I just do,' replied Roo mysteriously, and then grinned. 'I said, "Do you want to fly, Attlee?" and he got up and followed me.'

She sat down with the others, with the cat on her lap, and Rosanna struck a match.

'Here goes,' she said, and she lit the wick and spoke the wish in a bright, unsteady voice.

CHAPTER 36

Ed's first impression was that he'd been jammed into a tiny, dark room with four other people – four other people with enormous arms and shrill voices. There was only one source of light, a hole through which a patch of blue was visible above a bunch of jostling heads, and although the only noises were squeaks, and all the heads looked alike and the arms weren't arms but wings, Ed somehow knew that he was wedged in between Willard and Roo, with Rosanna just behind them and Attlee shoving his way to the front, actually climbing over Ed's head to get there, his sharp little clawed feet digging in, his pointed wings hitting Willard and Roo in their beaked faces, his squeaks frantic with eagerness. The sky, whizzing with dark specks, momentarily disappeared as Attlee's narrow body filled the opening, and then he was gone – a curve of wings and a forked tail disappearing into the blue.

Ed scrambled up onto the edge of the nest, just ahead of Roo and Willard and saw a view that was larger than any he'd ever seen – a smear of land far beneath, and a sky that filled the whole of the rest of the world. He teetered on the edge, and then Willard surged forward, jostling him, and he fell . . . upwards. *He fell upwards.* The air lifted him as if he was on the outstretched hand of an invisible giant and he felt no sense of fear or danger – he knew that he couldn't drop out of the sky because he was almost a part of it, his body slicing perfectly through the air, the tiniest movement of his wings sending him curving in a different direction, the breeze flowing like warm water over his head. Every single bit of him knew exactly what to do and exactly how to do it. And the *speed* of it! Even when he'd been able to run, he'd never run this fast. He yelled with excitement, and heard the yell emerge as a thin, wild, scream, the high-sky noise of summer swifts, and another scream answered him as Roo zipped by. Ed swept in a wide circle and saw, as he passed, that in the nest he'd leaped from – just a cup of mud and grass under the gutter of a house – there was still a single fledgling, perched on the edge, wings fluttering, feet still gripping on, head bobbing uneasily.

'Go *on*, Rosanna,' shouted Ed, though there were no real words, just that thrilling scream, and then he dived upwards again, into a sky without end, and there was Attlee, chasing other swifts as if he hadn't realized that he was one too, and Willard tilting into a tight curve, like a racing yacht in a fierce wind; Ed wove zestfully between them and then plunged down again towards the nest.

Rosanna was still there, still hesitating, still swaying on the brink. Ed banked steeply and wheeled past, screaming, 'GO ON!' and saw, out of the corner of his eye, Rosanna flex her wings one more time before she tipped forward into the blue air and—

They were back. The light and the lightness were gone, the speed and the dazzle of it, and they were sitting round a dining-room table, in the middle of which was a dish containing a drawing pin and a blob of grease.

'Oh,' said Roo, in a sort of gasp, as if she'd just surfaced after an underwater swim. Attlee, still on Roo's lap, sat up, gave himself a brisk shake and then licked his lips, as if remembering a particularly delicious meal. Willard sat silently blinking, his expression dazed, then he lifted a hand, bunched the fingers together, and sent it into a wild dive.

'Whoosh,' he said softly. Ed opened his mouth to speak, and then closed it again. Some things were beyond words. He looked at Rosanna, who had almost missed her chance to fly at all, and to his surprise, she was smiling.

'I did it,' she said. 'I thought I wasn't going to be able to pluck up the courage, but I did it. I did it. I *jumped*.'

And that was that.

Except it wasn't.

CHAPTER 37

It was two weeks later, and Willard and Ed were on their way back from school.

'SLIME,' said Willard loudly, as they passed 41 Brent Avenue.

Over the past fortnight, they had developed a method of making the school journey more interesting by linking front-door colours to particular words, and taking turns to call them out as they passed. Slime (obviously) was green.

'The thing is,' said Ed, 'that what Mr Joshi doesn't tell you – BEETROOT – is that he's totally obsessed with old cars so that all his spelling tests—'

'ATTLEE HAIRBALL,' shouted Willard, as they

passed the brownish-black door of number 45.

'All his spelling tests,' continued Ed, 'have things like "ignition" in them, and "suspension". VERRUCA.'

They turned the corner into Ed's road and immediately spotted Roo standing at the front gate, looking out for them. Now that Ed and Willard went to school and back together, she had started going with her best friend Mina; they were both in the cross-country team, and they ran all the way, timing themselves.

'You've been ages,' she called out. 'Hurry up, something's happened. When I got in, Rosanna was in the living room with Mum and Dad, and they've all got strange expressions, but they won't tell me what's going on until you get back.' She was hopping up and down with anticipation. 'Please hurry!'

Ed headed for the front door.

'See you tomorrow, then,' said Willard quite loudly.

'What?' Ed looked back at him. 'No, you have to come too – you're part of anything to do with this.'

'Oh, OK,' said Willard cheerfully, following him in. 'I think so too, to be honest.'

The three grown-ups were in sitting in the living room. Ed and Roo's dad looked like a cartoon character who'd just been hit with a plank, while his mum kept taking deep breaths. Only Rosanna looked calm, if a bit pink in the face.

'Miss Filey has something to tell you,' said Ed's mum, sounding as if she'd just finished a half-marathon.

'Hello!' said Rosanna. 'Gosh, it's lovely to see you all. Yes, I've been doing a tremendous amount of thinking and I've come to a decision. I'm going to go travelling. My father left me some money, and I'm also going to sell most of the furniture in the house, and with the proceeds I'm going to go as far as I possibly can and for as long as I possibly can. Because' – she looked directly at Ed – 'because I never want to have to say, "I wish I'd done that when I had the chance".' Ed gave her a thumbs up, and she smiled back.

'But what's going to happen to Attlee?' asked Roo. 'Can we look after him?'

'I would love you to,' said Rosanna. 'The only trouble is that I don't think he'd be very happy if he had to move somewhere unfamiliar. So, that was the other part of my plan . . .' She looked over at Ed's mum and dad. 'May I tell them?' His dad was still looking like a stuffed animal, but his mother opened her mouth, closed it again, and then nodded. 'So,' said Rosanna, 'I wondered if you'd like to move in with Attlee. You and the whole family.'

'Into your house?' asked Roo.

'Well, it's technically your house now. I've changed my will to leave it to you and Ed, so you'd just be getting it somewhat early. All I'd ask for is one room set aside for me to stay in between trips, but that still leaves plenty of space – after all, it's much, much too big for one person and a cat.'

Ed felt as if his cramped living room, so stuffed with people and furniture that it was more of an obstacle course than a room, had suddenly expanded, the walls moving back, the air and light flooding in. It was like the start of another wish – but a wish that wasn't three minutes long, or even an hour or more, but permanent.

'Your house?' said Ed faintly.

'*Your* house,' repeated Rosanna firmly.

'So, you'd be living at the bottom of my garden?' asked Willard, thunderstruck.

'Would we?' asked Ed, looking at his parents. 'Can we?'

His mum and dad exchanged a glance.

'As long as that's what you both want,' said his mum.

'*Yes*,' said Roo very quickly.

'Ed?' asked his dad, when Ed didn't answer.

'Well, *duh*!' said Ed. He caught sight of Rosanna's puzzled expression. 'Sorry, that means "yes",' he said.

'It means yes thank you, it means yes please, it means yes definitely. Definitely. Definitely.'

'What it means,' said Willard, giving a celebratory leap, 'is that we'll practically be living in the same house and I can just climb over the back wall *whenever I want!*' He high-fived Ed, and then Roo, and then Rosanna, and then Ed and Roo's mum and dad, and then Ed again, and then he leaped up, said, 'I've got to tell my mum!' and sprinted out of the house.

For a moment or two there was silence.

Roo looked at Rosanna. 'Where will you go first?' she asked.

Rosanna grinned.

'Anywhere,' she said. *'Everywhere.'*

Also available by Lissa Evans

Small Change for Stuart

And the brilliant sequel,
Big Change for Stuart

David Fickling Books

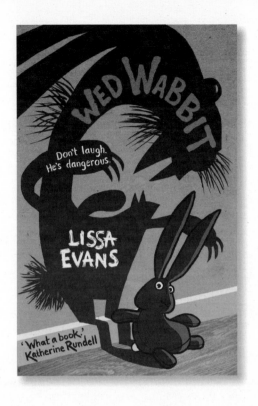

'So **funny** and so sharp and dark and **beautiful** and unguessable. What a book!' Katherine Rundell

'A future classic – **really really** funny' Nina Stibbe

'*Wed Wabbit* is a **classic** in the making' *The Times*

'A **riotously funny** adventure tale' *Observer*

Read on for a short extract from Lissa Evans' bestselling *Wed Wabbit*

ONE

It was such an ordinary evening, but every detail of it would matter; every detail would become *vital*.

'Wimbley Woos,' Minnie was wailing from her side of the bedroom. 'Wead me Wimbley Woos!'

'In a minute,' said Fidge. 'You're supposed to be drinking your milk.'

'But it's all warm and it's got a skin on top and it's *wevolting*.'

'All right, I won't be long.'

Fidge was packing. In just under thirty-six hours, her mother, her sister (aged four) and herself (aged ten and a half) were due to go on what was likely to be their best holiday for years and she wanted to be ready. She also wanted to try out a high-density packing technique she'd seen on a programme about mountaineers. What you did was roll up each item of clothing into an incredibly tight sausage, secured with an elastic band; you then fitted the sausages in next to each other, like a bundle of sticks. Fidge was going to attempt to put her entire holiday wardrobe into the very small backpack she used for school lunches. This was partly because she liked a challenge, and partly because she knew that her mother's luggage would (as usual) consist of a huge assortment of random bags, while Minnie never went anywhere without an armful of toys, which she then dropped at five-second intervals. *Somebody* had to have both arms free for emergencies.

'Wead me Wimbley Woos. Pleeeeeeease.'

'Not Wimbley Woos *again*. Ask Mum.'

'Sorry, Fidge, I can't,' called her mother from the living room, 'I've got to finish making this hat by tomorrow morning, it's for a bride's mother and she's terribly fussy.'

Fidge groaned and got to her feet.

Her sister's side of the room was spectacularly untidy. As Fidge picked her way across to the bed there was a loud squeak.

'Don't twead on Eleanor!' screamed Minnie.

'Well, don't leave her lying on the floor,' said Fidge, irritably. She stooped to pick up Eleanor, who was a purple elephant with a pink skirt, huge long pink eyelashes and a pink fluffy hair-do.

'She's asleep,' said Minnie. 'Wed Wabbit made them all go to bed early because they'd been naughty.'

2

'Oh.' Fidge looked down and realized that the teddies and dolls had been arranged in long rows, as if in a dormitory. Even the dolls' buggy was lying on its side, covered with a blanket; next to it, a silver bus with pink wheels had a little pillow under its front bumper. As usual, only Wed Wabbit was in bed with Minnie.

'OK,' sighed Fidge, sitting on the bed and plopping the elephant down beside her. 'You sure you want this book? We must have read it eight million times.'

'I want it.'

'How about I just read two pages?'

'No.'

'Five pages?'

'Mum! Fidge is being mean!'

'*Please* Fidge, just read her the whole book, it's not that long,' called their mother, sounding weary.

Fidge pulled a face, opened *The Land of Wimbley Woos* and started to read the horribly familiar lines.

'In Wimbley Land live Wimbley Woos
Who come in many different hues
In Yellow, Pink and Green and Blue
In Orange, Grey and Purple too.'

The first picture showed a group of happy-looking Wimblies. Each was a different colour, but they were all shaped like dustbins with large round eyes and short arms and legs, and

3

they radiated a sort of idiotic jollity. Fidge turned the page and continued reading in a bored, rapid mutter.

'Yellow are timid, Blue are strong
Grey are wise and rarely wrong
Green are daring, Pink give cuddles
Orange are silly and get in muddles.
Purple Wimblies understand
The past and future of our land.'

'Wead it pwoply, with *expwession,*' commanded Minnie, who could almost certainly pronounce the letter 'r' if she really tried, but who was too used to people going 'ohhhhhhh, how cuuuuuuuute' whenever she spoke, to want to make the effort.

Fidge carried on reading, with a fraction more feeling.

'Many talents make a team
So Wimbley Woos can build their dream
By sharing skills, plans, gifts and arts
And caring for each other's farts.'

'It's not "farts"!' shouted Minnie, outraged. 'It's *"caring for each other's* HEARTS".'

'If you know it that well then you don't need me to read it to you, do you?'

'But Wed Wabbit wants to hear it too.'

'Does he?' Fidge looked at Wed Wabbit, who was sitting

next to Minnie. He was very large and made of maroon velvet, with huge stiff ears, long, drooping arms and legs and tiny black eyes. He was her sister's favourite toy, bought from a charity shop two and a half years ago, just a week after their father died. Minnie had spotted the rabbit in the shop window and had darted in and wrapped her arms round him and hadn't let go. He'd been her favourite toy ever since, but perhaps because the awfulness of that week still sat like a weight on Fidge's head, she'd never liked Wed Wabbit. Most soft toys (in Fidge's experience) looked either smiley or sad, but Wed Wabbit had a horribly smug expression, like a clever child who knows he's the teacher's favourite and never, ever gets told off. She avoided his gaze and turned the page to an illustration of a group of Wimbley Woos scratching their heads.

'Oh, here's the bit where they try to think of a birthday present for the King of the Wimblies,' she said, with fake excitement. 'I wonder what they'll come up with? Dinner for two at a top sushi restaurant? A personalized number plate?'

'Wead it to me.'

'A spa weekend?'

'Please,' said Minnie, placing a small hand on Fidge's arm. '*Please* wead my book.'

And because Minnie (when she wasn't showing off, or being annoying or screechy or whiny) was really quite sweet, Fidge stopped mucking around and read the whole of it.

For the eight millionth time.

Over the course of twenty irritating pages the Wimbley

Woos organized a huge game of hide and seek as their surprise gift for the King, had a big celebration picnic, and sang their deeply soppy Wimbley Woo song as the sun set behind the lollipop-shaped trees of Wimbley Land.

'Wimbley Woo! Wimbley Woo!
Pink and Green and Grey and Blue
Yellow and Orange and Purple too
A rainbow of sharing in all we do!'

Fidge turned the page and looked at the last picture. It showed a mixed crowd of Wimblies standing on a hill looking up at the moon. At some point, Minnie had drawn a moustache on all the purple ones.

Minnie herself was almost asleep. Fidge tucked her in, slid the book onto the cluttered bedside table and then snatched it up again; amongst the junk was a small carton of juice and it was now on its side, and a pool of orange was spreading over the table top. Hastily, Fidge picked up the carton and then looked around for something to blot the juice with. Wed Wabbit seemed to catch her eye, his smirk as infuriating as ever, and before she knew what she was doing, she'd grabbed him by the ears and was pressing him down onto the spill. The effect was miraculous: Wed Wabbit acted like a huge sponge. The pool shrank steadily and then disappeared without trace, the orange making no stain at all on the dark-red velvet. Fidge, feeling relieved but a bit guilty, checked that

Minnie was definitely asleep, and then sat Wed Wabbit on the radiator and went back to her packing.

They were going on an outdoor activities holiday. Her mother and Minnie were going to potter round and play in the children's pool and Fidge was going to learn how to canoe, dive, abseil, climb, navigate, pot-hole and go-cart. She took an old T-shirt from the drawer and began to roll it very, very tightly. She had to leave enough space for the flippers her mother had promised to buy her.

It wasn't until the next afternoon that the terrible thing happened.